The Stones and the Stars

MORGAN BIRCH

Matador
9 Priory Business Park,
Wistow Road, Kibworth Beauchamp,
Leicestershire LE8 0RX
Tel: 0116 279 2299
Email: books@troubador.co.uk
Web: www.troubador.co.uk/matador
Twitter: @matadorbooks

ISBN 978 1788038 102

British Library Cataloguing in Publication Data.
A catalogue record for this book is available from the British Library.

Printed and bound in the UK by 4edge Limited
Typeset in 11pt Minion Pro by Troubador Publishing Ltd, Leicester, UK

Matador is an imprint of Troubador Publishing Ltd

To Jacob, Frances,
Nina and Emily

PROLOGUE

"It is them must find Her, them and no others."

The words hung in the air for a second, then dropped into the minds of the waiting Gypsies like a stone into a well. Eyes widened, breath was drawn in sharply and thoughts showed plainly on three familiar faces.

Them! Gaujos! What have them to do with the King?

Pigsticker looked around at his companions and held his peace for several moments to let the ripples settle. He knew that questions would come, so he lit his pipe and waited for them. He did not have long to wait. Tinman spoke first, his voice strained and tight from passion only barely held back.

"In all the years there ever was, Pigsticker, She has never trusted herself to a gaujo hand. 'Tis not right! How can it be?"

His hands curled into fists at his sides and the veins began to show in his powerful neck and arms. He ran out of words and simply looked at his old friend, confused and horrified beyond speech. Pigsticker didn't reply.

Mother Bessamy was next to speak.

"Never before has it been this way, that we know. I ask you all – if they are to find Her, what then? Must they also have a part in the Joining? And if they do not find Her, or do not consent to Give – what then? I fear the times that should follow on such a failing. All could be lost, and all protection against the Dark Times be gone. What then, I asks, what then?"

Again, Pigsticker gave no reply. He watched as Mother Bessamy's lined old face puckered in deep and troubled thought. She did not doubt the words, as she had Seen for herself in the dark glass that was her way of Knowing. But it was a hard truth and one that would require long thought, which time did not truly permit. Accustomed to Knowing, Mother Bessamy was, for once, at a loss.

Silence fell, and Pigsticker looked to the last of the company, who had not yet given her thoughts on the matter.

"Willow," he said softly, "what does you be saying?"

Willow's hazel eyes returned from the far distance where they had been searching. They held her companions one by one in their steady, warm gaze. A faint smile crept onto her face, at odds with the tear that ran down one freckled cheek. Finally, she spoke.

"Dark Times shall come indeed," she began, and a small shiver ran down Tinman's back as he recognised that she, too, had Seen. "Dark Times for all this world… and not so far away neither."

Pigsticker bowed his head, feeling the deep Rightness of her words as her calm voice went on:

"Dark Times we cannot halt nor even stall. Ours is only to set the foot on the path, be it the foot of friend or stranger. This Joining is an early step and it must come about, for without this beginning, there can be no Journey and no End. The task of the Joining falls to them, and though we know not why, 'tis us must help them. If we does not, all will be lost."

Once again the company was silent. Tinman bit back his protests, knowing that Willow's words had drawn them all into an unspoken agreement. He knew in his heart that now it was made, it could not be undone.

"So!" Pigsticker exclaimed, tapping out his pipe and returning it to one of his cavernous pockets, "'Tis agreed. If She should cross the path of the gaujos let us hope they has the sense to take Her in – and let us hope they will do what is needful in good time. I shall set the watchers on them while we makes ready all that we may."

And with that, Pigsticker nodded to his companions and headed off among the trees, blending easily into the undergrowth until he was invisible to all but the sharpest of eyes. Mother Bessamy, sprightly despite her age, linked arms with Willow and the two made their way swiftly out of the clearing. As she went, the old lady clicked her tongue to her small, shaggy dog, who came trotting in from the bushes, bits of grass and twigs hanging from his rough fur. He took up his place at her heel and snuffled along behind.

Tinman could do nothing but follow, leaving his anger behind him in the wood – for it was heavy to carry, and not likely to be of any use.

CHAPTER 1

Have to go and see the Pilchard. Mustn't forget. Fifteen minutes, then to the village, ask him to come and see Father. Mustn't forget.

On the very verge of sleep, Thomas Warrington thought dreamy thoughts and stretched like a cat on the springy grass. He closed his eyes against the sunlight that flashed between the tangled branches above. As his head filled with a dim glow of wavering red and green, the sounds outside grew fainter, as if the voices and the clinking and scraping of tools on rock were fading into the distance. The errand to the village was not urgent, and he knew that Gilbert would be there to remind him about it when the time came. He could always be relied on for things like that. 'Reliable' could have been Gilbert's middle name. Gilbert Reliable Warrington. GRW on his monogrammed notebook.

Tom had woken that morning to greyish-white light seeping through the faded canvas of his small tent and the sound of the birds singing in the dawn. His father and brother, each in tents of their own nearby, were also awake early. Tom had heard the Professor call to the students in their own larger tent, warning them that work was due to start. They had emerged, moaning over the hardships of camping, which had made Tom smile. Even with the early starts, this trip was one of the most comfortable he could remember. Last summer he had been bruised all over by stones under his groundsheet on Dartmoor, while the year before, the burning sun of Miklos had reddened his skin to blisters – all so that his father could search the earth for the treasures and trinkets which meant so much to him.

All of Tom's life had been shaped by his father's quest for knowledge about the past. His sole desire was to bring ancient objects to light and piece together the stories of how they had come to be. The Professor's feelings about his work were like the weather; they affected everyone around them and could change just as suddenly. When a precious artefact was found – a gold torc emerging from sticky mud or a piece of pottery from arid sands – it was as though the sun shone on them all. But when what emerged did not please him, the Professor's face became thunderous and everyone avoided his eye for fear of the temper-squall they may let loose.

But however the Professor's moods might vary, always, in the background, was one constant. The steady, monotonous voice of Gilbert was ever-present, describing, listing, cataloguing the finds, comparing them, numbering them, reading countless snippets from myriad books, creating order out of the muddle of the past. Like the rushing of the sea, it could be ignored, but its absence would leave an awful void.

Tom's job was simply to be as helpful as he could to the archaeological team as they went about their work. While the Professor and his students scraped carefully away at the earth with their various tools, lifting out occasional fragments of metal, pottery or bone, Tom fetched and carried and ran with messages from one end of the site to the other. He enjoyed the work, mostly. But now, for once, he was glad of a break. A sneaked swig or two from the students' cool stone cider jar had left him half-asleep on the grass. Father had tutted over this and called out, "One quarter-hour only, Thomas!" as he himself strode off back to the site with Gilbert, who, like him, hardly ever seemed tired.

"Thomas! Wake up!"

Tom scrambled at once onto his feet, his heart racing.

"Oh, it's you," he breathed, relieved at the sight of his brother Gilbert standing over him, his pocket watch in his hand. Father would have been angry, but Gilbert rarely seemed to mind what Tom did. He stood looking intently at the watch, which was one of his favourite things.

"You have been lying here for nineteen minutes," Gilbert announced, "when Father said you would only be resting for a quarter of an hour. He sent me to remind you that he needs you to go to the village and find the Pilchard, because Father wants to show him some new calculations that he has done. He thinks they might be quite significant. He wants you to go because he cannot leave the students and I will be busy with the measuring and John cannot go because he is working on the lower levels of the west quarter and…"

"Yes! Stop! I understand!" said Tom, clearly and firmly, putting up his hand to stem the flow of words. You sometimes had to do this with Gilbert, or else he would carry on explaining every detail until the person listening wanted to stick their fingers in their ears and scream.

Gilbert was not offended. "Oh," he said, "good." Then he added, with a faint smile, "I called him the Pilchard – that's funny…"

"Yes. I understand," said Tom, before Gilbert could explain further. Then he gave Gilbert a look of mock disapproval.

"You should show more respect," he advised in his best copy of their father's voice, wagging his finger. "Reverend Tobias Pilcher is a long-standing friend of mine, a scholar and a man of God, and your name for him is most improper!"

This was an act they had been through several times before, and Gilbert understood the joke well. He chuckled for a moment, then, without another word, turned and trudged off towards the site. Tom heaved himself onto his feet and set off for the village, to find the vicar and bring him to see the new calculations, though what they might prove, Tom had no idea.

Funny how Gilbert still laughs at jokes even when he's heard them a dozen times. One of his funny ways. Like being so exact about everything; what he's doing when, where all his things are and such. Like panicking if he loses a shirt-button or Father changes a plan. Saying the date each morning as if it was some kind of special day. Haven't had one of those for a long time. I wish something would happen... something exciting...

Tom's feet knew their own way to the village, having been that way many times. The path wound its narrow way out of the wood, then down a long slope and through a mass of bramble bushes and nettles. This was the only nasty part of the walk, where the prickles reached out to snag an unwary walker's shirt and mean little stingers raised burning white lumps on any skin they could touch. This time, Tom emerged unscathed from the bushes to walk out across the common land, where the grass was cropped short by the villagers' sheep and spotted with the droppings of the evening's rabbits.

Tom reached down to pick a long strand of grass, biting its end to taste the wild freshness of the sap. He then walked on towards the stile that nestled in the hedge surrounding the village fields. He sped up as he drew nearer to it, calculating his run-up, determined not to be beaten as he had been the last three times. Bounding the last few strides, he vaulted right over it, first go. Grinning in triumph, he ran downhill along the edge of the field, keeping off the ripening barley that turned the field to a mass of rolling green-gold waves. Finally, panting and red-faced, he reached the road.

The narrow road, hoof-printed and wheel-scarred, was lumpy and dusty in the summer heat. Tom treated its ridges as stepping stones, leaping and balancing as if they were narrow bridges over deep and dangerous chasms. He was so taken up with this that he didn't notice when he reached the village smithy and was almost past it before he realised that the blacksmith, Mr Moss, was calling to him.

"Thomas! Master Thomas Warrington! Bring that dreamy head of yours over here!"

Tom turned around to see the bearded, leather-aproned figure of Mr Moss standing beckoning to him. He was holding out a package for Tom to collect. Smoothing a hand over his sweaty, sticking-up hair, Tom trotted over to claim it.

"Sorry, Mr Moss, I was miles away!" he said, breathless from exertion and heat.

"Planning some mischief or other, I'd wager," the

smith replied, winking at Tom beneath his thick, bushy eyebrows. "But, see now, take this back to your dad, and tell him I've mended his fairy tools for him. Them new handles should last a good hundred years, tell him, and he should be able to dig up all sorts of bits and bobs and who-knows-what with 'em now, though that brush has seen better days. It needs a new head really and truly – a bit like a few folks I could mention, naming no names!"

"Thanks, Mr Moss," said Tom, putting the parcel of tools under his arm, "but I haven't got any money with me…"

"Don't let that bother your head," the smith replied, "I'll see your dad one of these days. Just so long as he don't try to pay me with fairy gold, we'll all be right."

With a short laugh and a nod, Mr Moss turned away, to where a farm horse was being led up to the forge, ready for shoeing. Though he would like to have stayed to watch, Tom headed back to the road, making for the vicarage to find the Pilchard. *Reverend Pilcher*, he corrected himself, firmly.

A few minutes later, Tom was standing in the vicarage garden with his father's old friend, who was pleased to see him. Tom had found him standing under a large tree whose every branch bent downwards under the weight of a mass of apples.

"What do you think of that, Thomas?' the vicar asked, pointing at the enormous crop. "Have you ever seen such abundance? 'Be fruitful and multiply' seems to be the text for the day, don't you think?"

"What will you do with all those?" asked Tom, staring open-mouthed at the fruit crammed onto the branches.

"I shall give them away to anybody who needs them, of course," said Reverend Pilcher, smiling. "But here's an interesting thing, Thomas. That tree has never fruited like this in all my years in this village. But then, the year before last, your friend the Gypsy gentleman came by and he saw that the crop was rather dismal. He did some pruning for me and by next May-time there was more blossom than I'd ever seen in my life! And now, this wonderful abundance! Like a miracle, almost, Thomas!"

Reverend Pilcher smiled down broadly at Tom. Then the two set off promptly back to the wood, for the vicar was eager to see whatever the Professor wanted to show him at the archaeological site.

All the way back up the road, along the edges of the fields, across the common land and on towards the wood, Reverend Pilcher chatted away about local history and landmarks. He always said that, after the Church, the past was his greatest passion, and it was because of Reverend Pilcher that the archaeological dig had started in the first place. He had suspected for a long time that the wood held a secret or two, as he put it, and his own research had led him to consider that the place had been important in ancient times.

"I have reason to believe that the standing stones may have had a religious purpose," he had said to Professor Warrington when they first talked about it. "Pre-Christian, of course, but not pre-God, presumably."

This had sent the Professor into a flurry of excitement. Eventually his interest had brought them all here, to try to discover the meaning of the jagged ring of stones that had stood there for so long. Something lurked below, the two men were sure. Something, they hoped, of great interest and worth. They had found a reference to a 'King-stone' hidden among the silverfish in a dusty book from 1744. Entitled *Curiosities of the Marches* and written by one Reverend Silas Pinchbrow, the old book had set them off on the kind of quest that the Professor could never resist.

As they approached the wood, Reverend Pilcher stopped for a moment to rest his long, skinny legs after the long walk up the slope. He looked all around, struck by the fine views from the top.

"God's creation, Thomas," he said, staring into the distance, "which He gave over into mankind's care. And yet, not all of mankind can be trusted with it. If a certain local gentleman has his way, this wood may not be here much longer, you know. Mr Montfalcon fully intends to clear this land, to sell off the timber and then have a road built through, to connect his house to his place of business. How can a person not see the beauty of this place, Thomas? How can he see it as an obstacle, something to dispose of because it is not convenient?"

"I don't know," replied Tom, who had been disgusted when he first heard Mr Montfalcon's plans. "I don't like to see trees cut down, and once when we saw some birches being felled, it upset Gilbert so much that he threw himself down on the ground and cried."

"Thanks be to God for sensitive souls!" exclaimed Reverend Pilcher. "Because this world needs them. The meek shall inherit the Earth, so the Bible tells us. But come," he said, looking down at Tom, "let us take those tools to your father. I expect you've heard enough verses and sermons for one day."

When they arrived at the site, the atmosphere was heavy with dread. Professor Warrington was nowhere to be seen and the students were working quietly, heads down, as if trying not to draw attention to themselves. John, the youngest of them, looked up as he saw the two figures approaching the edge of the excavations and made a warning kind of face. Silently, he pointed to the largest of the tents. This was the store, where the finds were examined, laid out and labelled, before being packed carefully into crates, ready to be taken away.

Tom knew exactly what the trouble would be. Father and Gilbert were having one of their rows. Just now and then, there would be an angry explosion as Professor Warrington's fervour met Gilbert's doggedness head-on, setting off rounds of thunderous rage and dangerous silence. Sure enough, their voices suddenly sounded through the canvas and Tom winced, knowing what was to come.

"Gilbert, for heaven's sake!" Father bellowed. "We have not got time for this! Just get on with what I asked you to do and do not take so infernally long about it! Have you forgotten that time is against us? Do you think we have all year? A month, Gilbert – that is all we have left before this site is lost to us forever! So no more delays! We just cannot afford them!"

Tom could imagine Gilbert's distress at hearing this tirade, and he knew that his brother would not be able to answer it. Sure enough, no words came in reply, just a loud cry; a harsh droning sound that Tom had heard many times before. He could picture Gilbert standing as he always did at times like these, with his eyes shut tight, his fists clenched and his bent arms covering his ears, rocking to and fro, making that sound over and over again. Reverend Pilcher looked at Tom, with both alarm and pity all over his face.

"It's not as bad as it sounds, sir," Tom told him. "That's how Gilbert goes when he gets upset by things. He does it to drown the voices out, I think. He just can't stand being shouted at, and being hurried always makes him panic. He hates it."

Just then, Professor Warrington burst out of the tent and stormed away, leaving the students watching uneasily.

"Same old Ronald," murmured Reverend Pilcher, "he always was full of fire. I'll go after him in a moment or two. Thomas, will you see to your brother?"

"It's best to leave him for a while," Tom advised, from long experience. "I'll talk to him later, but he needs time on his own to calm down first."

The vicar nodded kindly then set off to catch up with his old friend. Tom walked away towards the edge of the wood, kicking at the grass rather moodily as he went. Turning his back on the camp, he stood alone beside a clump of tall bushes, shredding a leaf in his fingers and feeling that the day was ruined.

Then, to his utter surprise, he was whisked into the bushes by a long, strong arm that shot out with no warning at all. The owner of the arm laughed out loud, delighted at the surprise on the boy's face.

"Pigsticker!" exclaimed Tom.

CHAPTER 2

"The very same," came the reply. Tom grinned, seeing the familiar figure in his old earth-coloured clothes and dilapidated felt hat. Two lively, dark eyes peered out from under the fraying brim.

"Pardon me, Master Thomas," Pigsticker continued, the country burr strong in his voice, "but I needs the help of a strong young man for a most important job that can't wait."

"I'll help," said Tom, pleased to have a reason to stay away from the site. "What job is it?"

But Pigsticker had already set off on the unknown mission, shambling through the undergrowth as if just wandering away. Tom followed him, ducking down to avoid low-growing boughs, pushing aside wandering stems that whipped back as he passed, then swishing through bracken that grew waist-high. For all that he seemed to be dawdling along, Pigsticker moved with surprising speed, leaving Tom trailing. He now seemed to be following a definite route, yet when Tom looked back over his shoulder, he could see no mark of their passing at all.

"Where are we going?" called Tom, trying to catch up.

Pigsticker stopped for a moment to turn round slowly.

"Those that asks no questions don't get told no lies," he said, tapping the side of his nose with a finger that looked rather like a knobbly root. Then he trudged off again and Tom, none the wiser, scrambled along behind.

Deeper in the wood, the hot sun was muted by the shade of the trees. Dappled sunlight shone through the leaves, clouds of gnats danced in the shafts of light and here and there, brown speckled butterflies flitted over the ferns in search of flowers. Pigsticker forged ahead, following a path that could barely be seen among the bushes and bracken. After a time, the old Gypsy and his young companion emerged into a glade where several of the faint paths met, beside a huge oak tree. Tom stopped under the tree to stare, open-mouthed, up into its vast, spreading branches.

That's the biggest tree I've ever seen! How old must it be?

"I knew this 'un when it were nothing but an acorn," Pigsticker said, his eyes twinkling.

He chuckled to himself for a moment, and the sound of his laugh was echoed by the hammering of a woodpecker, somewhere out of sight among the trees.

That tree is at least a hundred years old! How could he have known it…?

"You any good with ladders?"

Pigsticker's question cut through Tom's wondering.

"Ladders?" Tom was confused. "I suppose so, why?"

Pigsticker turned to look him up and down.

"Holding a ladder," he said, "is a very responsible job. Only to be entrusted to a safe pair of hands."

"Er… yes, it would be," Tom agreed, still uncertain of what was going on. Pigsticker gave nothing away.

The bees, always tell the bees anything that's important, or might be. Tell 'em, show ' em, make sure they knows all they needs to know. Don't leave 'em out, oh, dear, no. Tell 'em what's what and you can trust they'll do right.

Five minutes later, the two of them stood looking up at a beech tree with rich, deep-green leaves.

"Up there," Pigsticker asserted, "is the finest honey you'll ever taste. We just need to climb up and ask the bees for a comb or two."

Winking at Tom, he suddenly trudged off into a dense patch of undergrowth. Moments later, he re-emerged, with a few twigs and a stray cobweb clinging to his hat and waistcoat. There was a rough ladder over his shoulder, covered with moss and missing a rung or two. It looked unlikely to bear his weight, but he leaned it against the tree and Tom held it so he could climb up. Slowly, he scaled the rickety rungs, then hoisted himself onto a sturdy branch, where he sat, calmly waiting.

I hope Pigsticker knows what he's doing... he could get stung to death!

Down at the foot of the ladder, peering up into the branches, Tom crossed his fingers and then his toes. It was an uncomfortable way to attract luck and Gilbert had often told him off for superstition, but he did it nonetheless. He could hear a low buzzing coming from the heart of the beech tree and see a few bees flying curiously round Pigsticker's head. He was sitting close to the trunk and seemed to be whispering into the nest. Tom listened intently to the sound, which had something in common with the bees' own hum as well as the sighing of the wind and the rustle of the leaves.

Slowly, Pigsticker rolled up his sleeve and reached deep into the tree. In a moment, he pulled out a gleaming piece of honeycomb as big as two fists. This he placed carefully in his hat. Then, with a final word to the bees, he climbed one-handed down the ancient ladder and, without a word, held out the hat to Tom.

Tom stared at the honeycomb in astonishment. It seemed to glisten like melting gold and the air was thick with the sweet smell of it. As the last couple of bees launched themselves off it, he scooped up some of the golden honey and licked it off his finger. It was the most delicious thing he had ever tasted.

"Not bad," was Pigsticker's comment, as he too tasted some.

He fished in one of his many pockets and brought out a piece of scruffy waxed paper, which he used to wrap a big chunk of honeycomb before handing it to Tom.

"Fair's fair, when you did half the work," he told him. He wrapped up his own piece in a dock leaf and stowed it somewhere inside his worn jacket. Then he put his hat back on, sticky as it was.

"Good for your hair, they say," he remarked, and certainly he did have a thick, black thatch despite his age and the hair had a faint sheen like a crow's feathers.

"Why didn't the bees sting you?" asked Tom, amazed by what he had seen.

"I asked 'em politely," Pigsticker replied, "and besides, them *pishoms* knows how I likes a bit of honey."

Then, after returning the ladder to its hiding place, he set off back towards the camp and once more, Tom hurried along behind.

There now. They knows. Let them make of it what they will. No doubt they'll do as they is bid.

As they drew near to the camp and the archaeological site, Pigsticker waited for Tom to catch up.

"Has you found anything yet?" he asked, casually. "Apart from the stones, that is, and I can't see they'd take much finding."

"Er… not really, but the excavation isn't finished yet," Tom told him.

"Excavation?" echoed Pigsticker, admiringly. "That's a fancy word. Digging, I calls it."

He rooted in his pockets for his pipe and sat down on a fallen tree, where he could just watch the camp through gaps in the greenery. He then filled the pipe with tobacco using comfortable, habitual movements.

"Grand invention, lucifers," he said, striking the match, "it were no easy task lighting a pipe with a tinder box…"

He puffed out some smoke, which hung like a wraith in a shaft of sunlight. Tom agreed that they were indeed a marvellous thing. He loved fire himself and was rarely without some candle ends and a few matches, which lived in the pocket of his trousers and waistcoat, among the bits of string, scraps of paper and general flotsam and jetsam that gathered there.

Gil once said that he would never dare put his hand into 'a pocket that could contain so many varieties of detritus'. Not like his, with just his watch, his pencil and his notebook… You never know what you might need, I say…

On the site, the Professor was directing two of the students as they worked with ropes and sextant.

"What are they up to now?" asked Pigsticker.

"They're measuring the distances between the stones and trying to work out if they line up with any local landmarks," said Tom, pleased to be able to answer. "Father thinks that stone circles weren't put up just any-old-where, but are in line with other things in the landscape – like a hill or another standing stone or something – so he's looking at the angles with a sextant."

"Oh, is that the way of it?" Pigsticker murmured, nodding.

"Yes," replied Tom, hoping that Pigsticker wouldn't ask how the sextant worked, as he had no idea. "Father thinks that the circle might be a kind of calendar, so it could be lined up with the sun, or the moon or the stars."

The old Gypsy raised one eyebrow.

"He's a clever one, that Professor," he said after a moment, through another cloud of smoke, "but he don't know much about circles. Circles is round, as even our young Cobby knows at four summers old, and them stones ain't nowhere near."

"Well," said Tom, not wanting his father to sound stupid, "circles don't have to be round. Erm… what I mean is… there's groups of standing stones all over Britain and they're not all round."

Tom stopped, realising that Pigsticker's eyes were twinkling again, as if he was trying not to laugh.

"I doubt there's many like the Maidens," was the old man's only comment.

"I can't believe Mr Montfalcon would cut a road through this wood," Tom said, in a sudden change of mood. "It's a rotten thing to do. He's even said that he might demolish the circle, depending on where the best route is for the road."

Pigsticker's face darkened.

"It's not rightfully his to destroy," he growled.

"But he says he owns the land, so he can do as he sees fit," Tom replied sadly. "Rich people can do anything they want."

Pigsticker scowled.

"Thinking like that will be the death of us all," he spat out, then stood up briskly and knocked out his pipe against the fallen tree.

"Come and eat with us tomorrow night," he called over his shoulder as he stumped away. "Bring that brother of yours. Tinman's wife will cook up a rabbit stew fit for a king!"

And then he was gone, leaving nothing behind but the echo of his bird-like whistling.

Imagine King Edward sitting down at his fancy table, with his guests and his servants and his silver dishes, and finding it's rabbit stew for dinner. Would he cut the cook's head off? Or would he just send it back and shout for something more fancy? He doesn't know what he's missing.

When Tom arrived back at the site, the whole place felt much more settled. The Professor and Reverend Pilcher, in a pair of old canvas chairs, were poring over Gilbert's red ledger.

"Most peculiar," the Pilchard was saying, "but time still remains, Ronald."

They barely noticed Tom as he walked past them, on his way to his own tent to put the honeycomb safe for later. But as he approached the family camp, his heart sank. There, sitting waiting for him, was his least favourite person in the world, Geraldine Montfalcon.

Geraldine had visited the site all summer, pretending to

be interested in the archaeology. Really, her intention had been to taunt and annoy Tom at every opportunity. Worse, she had quickly learned to spot Gilbert's quirks and make his life miserable. She did as she pleased, always safe in the knowledge that nobody could stand up to her father, and that adults found her charming. To cap it all, she was always horribly smart and clean and she made Tom uncomfortably aware of his own dusty, tousle-haired, grass-stained state.

"I thought I'd find you here, Tommy," she said, "once you got back from playing in the wood with that old tramp."

The name 'Tommy' grated on Tom's nerves, as did the description of Pigsticker, but he took a deep breath and tried not to show that he cared.

"Hello, Geraldine," he said, as politely as he could bear to.

Geraldine lifted the canvas flap and walked into Tom's tent.

"You don't mind if I come in, do you?" she said. Tom quickly squeezed past her, defensive of his small area of private space.

"It's not very big, is it?" Geraldine said scornfully, looking around. "Couldn't you afford a bigger tent?"

"It's only meant for one person," said Tom, pointedly. She ignored him.

"Still, things could be worse," she carried on, "at least you don't have to share with your mad brother. Where is he anyway? Out in Simpkin's meadow, counting the blades of grass? Trying to put the flowers into straight lines?"

Tom's eyes narrowed. "Gilbert's not mad," he replied through gritted teeth, "he's cleverer than you'll ever be."

"I expect he only seems mad to normal people," Geraldine said, airily.

She stared at Tom with her bright green eyes, then tossed her long, dark red hair and gave him a spiteful smile.

"Poor old Gilbert," Geraldine cooed in a voice of fake concern. "I've heard him, you know, in his tent, gibbering away to himself in his made-up language. What a ridiculous noise! Like talking backwards!"

"It's Welsh!" Tom said. "He likes to practise it sometimes, that's all."

"Welsh!" scoffed Geraldine. "Who on Earth would want to speak Welsh?"

"People in Wales, I should think," replied Tom, with a glare.

I'd like to knock her down, right now, and give her the hiding she deserves. But Father would go up like a volcano and Mr Montfalcon would throw us all off the site in an instant…

"So Giddy Gilbert pretends he's Welsh," she said, sounding interested.

"He's half-Welsh. So am I. Our mother was from Wales," Tom told her with angry pride.

Tom felt a pang of sadness at the mention of his mother. She had died when Tom was very young and now watched over them, serious-faced, from an oil painting in Father's study. The thought of her made Tom feel twisted up inside. He would have hated Geraldine to know.

"I suppose having Celtic blood has its compensations," she remarked, in a tone that set Tom's teeth on edge. "It gives you an excuse to speak a mad language and make friends with Gypsies and tramps. You do know that all those Romanies are thieves, don't you? Be sure to lock all your doors when they're about, my father says. Oh, but you don't have a door, do you? Well, remember anyway, they're nothing but common robbers, the lot of them. And don't get too close to any of them," at this point Geraldine lowered her voice delicately and added, "I'm sure they have *fleas* as well."

You stupid, ignorant girl. Those Gypsies are a hundred times better than you. At least they know how to treat people properly and they don't pick on people who can't defend themselves. They wouldn't take any nonsense from you, either, no matter who your fancy Papa might be.

Tom was saved from having to answer by the arrival of Professor Warrington, who called to him from outside the tent. Geraldine walked out to meet him, a sweet smile ready on her lips.

"Oh, Miss Montfalcon," the Professor said, a little embarrassed as he often was in female company, "how nice to see you. I hope Thomas has been looking after you well."

"Oh yes, Professor," she replied, "he's been telling me such interesting things about your work here. I'm sorry to leave, but sadly I must. My father will be waiting for me."

And she walked away, shaking out her hair behind her and turning to wave as she went.

"Hmm, I'm glad to see you've struck up a friendship there, Tom," said the Professor to his younger son. "But run along and find Gilbert for me, will you? I need him to check some measurements."

Friendship?! What? She's no friend of mine! If you

looked properly instead of always working, you'd see that she's horrible and a bully and... you don't even care, all you care about is the dig, the dig, the dig...

Before setting off in search of his brother, Tom glumly retrieved the honeycomb from its sticky paper wrapping and took a fair-sized bite. The sweetness almost managed to take away the bitter taste from his mouth.

CHAPTER 3

Later that evening, after supper, Tom and Gilbert sat together beside a small fire, watching the ever-changing pictures drawn by the flickering flames and talking over the events of the day. Unfortunately, it had been John's turn to cook supper that day, which was always a disaster. Tom had looked at his plateful with trepidation. Blackened sausages hiding as if ashamed under a mound of potato-and-bean mess, garnished with chunks of onion that were still half-raw but with burnt outsides. They looked like cockroach shells. He had manfully eaten the awful stuff, but it had proved hard to digest and his escaping belches had annoyed the Professor.

"I will not permit borborygmi at the table!" he had declared, forgetting for a moment that the meal was being eaten in the open air of the Marches and not in his stuffy, formal dining room. But wherever he was, his word was law and both Tom and Gilbert were banished to their own corner of the camp and their own small fire. Neither minded much; in fact, it was quite handy, as the two of them could eat the remaining honey without having to share it round.

"Horrible Geraldine was here earlier," Tom informed his brother. "She barged straight into my tent then told me it was too small – as if you couldn't see the size of it from the outside. Worse, Father came along and thought I was friends with her! Urgh!"

Tom made a vomiting sound as the only way to express his horror, then wished he hadn't, as it reminded him of the turbulence in his stomach.

"Yes, she was here for twenty-five minutes before you came back," Gilbert reported. "She was talking about a new camera which her father has given her and she said that she intends to bring it here and take some photographs. I tried to tell her that we had a full photographic record of the site already, but she just laughed and ran away."

That girl is extremely peculiar. She asks questions yet pays no attention to the answers. Even more illogically, she suggests an answer of her own which is ridiculous and impossible. She asks questions with no evident purpose. She asks questions in such rapid sequence that there can be no possibility of answering them. Time after time, I find myself reduced to silence and misery and confusion.

I hate her! How dare she pick on Gilbert? She has no idea. Why can't she just leave us alone?

"Was anything interesting found today?" Tom asked later, when he had placed a few more sticks on the fire and stirred it into sparks.

"It depends what you mean by 'interesting'," Gilbert told him, carefully. "There were seventeen fragments of ironstone pottery in the north trench. It is likely that they are the remains of a single cider cask and of no great significance. There was also what appeared to be a buckle from a shoe or maybe a boot. It was plain and of quite recent manufacture. There was also a sheep's shin bone, which may have been brought here and buried by a fox. Each item was correctly labelled and stored, although Father objected to time being spent on them… The main pit reached a depth of twelve feet at the deepest point, though rocks were a considerable obstacle..."

Tom listened to the monologue with one ear, as he did most evenings. Night had finally fallen and the small fire began to surrender to the darkness, its wavering orange light drawing back from the shadows at the edge of the trees. The murmuring voices of the Professor and his friend (who was to stay the night) could just be heard as they reminisced about times long gone. The students talked together and teased each other in their usual, familiar way. Tom yawned hugely and, as he closed his eyes, an owl hooted, the sound clear and close in the cool night air.

"Thomas!" for the second time that day, Gilbert's voice cut through Tom's dreaminess. "Do you want to see it or not?"

"Oh, er, yes, of course," Tom replied, shaking himself into the present moment and realising that he had lost track of what Gilbert was saying.

Tom expected to see his brother make for the tent where the finds were stored, each in its buff envelope or box lined with cotton wool, labelled in Gilbert's cramped, scratchy handwriting. But no; Gilbert stepped instead into his own tent and returned a moment later, holding his hands cupped in front of him. To Tom's surprise, his brother then knelt down carefully, bowed his head and murmured over the item in Welsh, in a soft voice not at all like his usual one.

Tom's Welsh was nowhere near as good as Gilbert's. "Gil," he asked, "what are you saying?"

Gilbert looked up, his eyes even more distant than usual. When he answered, his tone was solemn.

"That which was lost, now is found," he said.

Then he lowered his eyes again and stared at the object he held in his hands, as if he couldn't tear himself away.

What's going on? This is very odd. He looks like he's moonstruck.

"Well, what is it?" Tom asked.

At this, Gilbert jumped, startled like a sleeper suddenly woken. He dropped the treasure in front of Tom and stood for a moment, wide-eyed, flapping his hands in an agitated way and opening his mouth as if to speak, but no words came.

Concerned but curious, Tom finally took a look at the object which had dropped from Gilbert's hands. But if he had hoped for riches, for glinting gold or a fabulous jewel, he was to be disappointed. The thing was merely a stone, reddish in colour, about the size of a cricket ball. It was an odd shape, rather like a figure-of-eight; broad and rounded at the ends and thinner in the centre, like a lady's dress pulled in tightly at the waist.

"A rock," said Tom, reaching to take it in his hand.

But no, maybe it was not just a rock. Picking it up, Tom was amazed by its weight, which was far greater than its size suggested. There were traces of metal somehow mixed in with the stone, as if they had melted, flowed together and hardened into one. Tom turned to ask his brother what on Earth the thing was. But before he could say the words, he was shocked to feel the stone in his hands grow strangely warm, and for an instant he felt extremely peculiar. His whole body seemed to be swooping heavily downward then swinging up again, with starry blackness pressing hard against his closed eyes.

Then, all at once, the stone was cool and the moment passed, leaving Tom feeling faintly dizzy, as if he had just stepped off a fairground ride. Gilbert reached out to take the strange thing back.

"I've never seen anything like that before," Tom said to him, a little unsteadily.

"Neither have I," replied Gilbert, in his normal voice but more quiet than usual, "and, what is more, I have not added it to the catalogue."

What? He never leaves anything out of the catalogue.

"Does Father know about it?" Tom asked, with growing alarm.

"No," replied his brother, and in that one word, the stone was declared to be a secret.

Without further talk, Gilbert returned to his tent with the stone, and stayed there, leaving Tom confused and slightly worried, staring into the embers of the dying fire.

"Is all well, Thomas?" came a familiar voice out of the darkness. Tom looked up to see Reverend Pilcher standing over him, smiling and holding out a lit oil lamp.

"Oh, yes, thank you, sir," Tom replied, flustered, getting to his feet and hoping that he didn't look as if he'd been up to something. But if he did, the vicar didn't take note of it.

"I just thought you might like a lantern to light you to bed," he said softly, "your father has just retired for the night, but he asked me to come over and say goodnight to you both for him."

"Oh, erm, yes, thank you," said Tom, knowing this was unlikely to be true, as Father rarely bothered with such pleasantries.

Accepting the lamp, though he did have a candle and a

box of matches in his tent, Tom called a muted goodnight to the Reverend and ducked into his own small tent. He was indeed glad of the lamp's warm, calm glow, and sorry to douse it when he had climbed into his narrow camp bed.

Mist rose eerily from the damp forest floor. It drifted upwards in hazy spirals, disappearing into the air, only to re-form and rise again, glowing faintly against the blackness of the night. Walking slowly and alone through the swirling white vapour, Tom felt goosebumps rising and a shiver pass over his skin. A night bird screeched overhead and was answered by the yelping of a fox somewhere nearby. The trees stood majestically all around; vast, dark presences, spreading their branches far out and upward towards the distant stars.

Tom glided to a halt under the ancient boughs. As he stood, wide-eyed and silent, he became aware that he could just hear the leaves on the trees rustling lightly, almost as if they were whispering to each other, though there was not a trace of breeze. Under his bare feet, Tom could feel the roots of the trees, a web of branching fibres reaching deep down into the ground, pulsing slightly like arteries and veins under skin. All around, out of sight in the mist and the darkness, Tom felt the small forest creatures urgently scurrying. In contrast, he himself was motionless, suspended in time, waiting; but for what, he had no idea.

In front of him, Tom noticed that the mist was

beginning to thin out, leaving two wispy columns with a growing space between them. He drew in his breath expectantly, but as the mist parted it revealed only a badger, sitting there calmly regarding him through small, dark eyes in its black-and-white striped face. It looked at Tom for a long moment before turning tail and padding off, and the mist slowly closed back over the space where it had been. As Tom watched it go, the broad, pale form of a barn owl launched itself from a branch above his head. He felt the breeze of its feathered wings on his cheek and ruffling his hair as it swooped down past him then disappeared without a trace.

Still rooted to the spot, Tom began to be aware that the whispering of the trees was growing louder. Here and there amongst the sighing sounds, the whispers were almost words, though hushed and indistinct. He strained his ears to hear the language, but every time, it eluded him, leaving him feeling that he was grasping at something that hovered just out of his reach.

Tom tried to summon his own voice, wanting to call out into the dark, to ask who was speaking and what they were saying. But he soon found that his mouth would move only with a queer slowness and, though he tried and tried, no sound would emerge at all, leaving the questions just echoing vaguely in his mind. Then he watched, fascinated, as the mist began to move again, shaping itself before his eyes into vague, shadowy outlines. They wavered and flowed together then separated, then flowed together and separated again, and again, before finally drawing together into definite forms – the shapes of human figures...

GHOSTS!

Tom snapped awake and sat upright, his heart pounding furiously, every muscle tense with fright. For a few seconds, the fear held him tightly and he could neither move nor breathe. Then, slowly, cautiously, he dared to peer around. There was his familiar blanket, clutched tightly in his fists; there were the tent walls, sagging slightly inwards just as they always did, and his clothes lying in the heap where he had dropped them. The dark bulk that was his trunk… yes, everything was in its proper place, solid and ordinary and real.

As the fear drained away and his heartbeat slowly returned to normal, Tom breathed deeply and lay back down on his camp bed, pulling the blanket safely up around his chin. After a few more moments he yawned and sighed and closed his eyes, drifting back into sleep. This time he slept soundly, untroubled by shadowy figures or mysterious voices. He didn't wake again until the sun was lighting the sky and Gilbert's announcement of the date sounded out, to mark the beginning of another new day.

CHAPTER 4

Thursday, August the ninth, nineteen hundred and four. Eight shirt buttons, bottom to top. One – set out the ledger for the day's finds. Two – check with father that the main pit is to be dug a further foot in depth. Three – if not, hear new instructions and proceed accordingly. Four – ensure supplies of envelopes; and Five – open new bottle of ink. Six – and that which was lost is found. Wait, no. What? Stop. Go back. Unbutton. Start again. One…

Alone in his neat and tidy tent, Gilbert was dressing in his usual orderly fashion, using the buttons of his shirt and waistcoat almost like an abacus or a rosary. The steady, habitual action was his way of gathering his thoughts and planning his day. Usually it brought him great comfort, but this morning his head felt horribly untidy inside, all his thoughts mixed up like books badly shelved. He was forced to use the flat of his hand to slap his forehead seven times before he was able to work through his whole list in order. Only when the timetable was complete could he take up his ledger and march out onto the site to start work.

Outside, another busy day was beginning for Professor Warrington's archaeological team. Arthur cooked breakfast on the camping stove and tried not to curse as hot bacon fat spat onto his fingers. There was a little splashing of water in token efforts at washing, but not much more, for hauling buckets of water was becoming a major chore in the hot, dry weather. Bootlaces were tied, short walks taken to the plank-and-pit arrangement in the woods, well-worn clothes reluctantly buttoned up. Remarks were made about the hot weather and the day ahead, as they were every day.

And yet, all was not quite as it should have been. An uncomfortable tension hissed and hummed in the air and every member of the team could feel it. Silent voices whispered constantly of the threat to the site, the shortage of time, and most of all, the failure of modern archaeology to uncover the secrets of the ancient stones. Stubbornly, the site clung on to its mystery and wildness, resisting the ever-deeper delvings, the meticulous measuring, charting and diagram-making and all the team's knowledge of ring-stones anywhere in the world.

So, not knowing what else to do, the students, John, Wilfred, Cedric and Arthur, returned to their toil. For weeks now they had been digging down through the layers of earth in the centre of the ring and beyond, seeking any sign of the mythical King Stone. The hauled away the earth in wicker baskets, heaped it up and covered it with oilskins, trying not to think about how they must soon haul it all back. They took turns at working the new, outlying trenches and were at least glad that the Professor had called a halt to searching the woods for any sign of the stone.

The students would never forget the days they had spent in the woods. They had trudged for miles there, round and round, seeking clues but finding nothing; at first in torrential downpours and then, for better or worse, in the full heat of high summer. Their spirits had been high in the early days at the thought of a long camping holiday, but had waned over time. They had remarked ruefully to each other that mud, marching and trenches would be the death of them all.

While the students dug and searched and Gilbert catalogued and stored, Tom was kept busy as usual with his messages and errands. There were messages to deliver, tools or drinks to carry to the workers, lost items to be found and frayed ropes to be mended. His cheerful, flitting presence did more than he knew to lighten the mood of the camp. The students teased him mercilessly; sending him hunting for items that didn't exist, or giving him messages to pass on that turned out to be jokes on him. Tom would always get his own back in some small way and all enjoyed the foolery. The fact that it had to be kept out of the Professor's sight made it all the more fun.

Meanwhile, with his friend the vicar having left to tend his flock, the Professor sat gloomily in the canvas chair outside his tent. Sighing impatiently, he took up, for the hundredth time, the dog-eared and mildewed book that had brought him to this place. The book fell open at the page and, though he knew Reverend Pinchbrow's old-fashioned, pompous words by heart, he read them once again.

'The Megaliths designat'd by the appellative of the Nine Maids are a curious Formation that is unique in my Experience of such Structures, for they do form not a Circle, as was the typical

manner of the Ancients of these Isles, but an
altogether more perplexing Order…'

Skimming over the next paragraph or two, Professor thought back to his very first view of the stones. He and Pilcher had stood together under rainy skies and stared in quiet excitement at the waist-high wedges of hewn granite, knowing that they were a rich mystery ripe for the unravelling. Some of the stones stood strongly upright, some had fallen flat to nestle in the grass, forming a loose ring with a peculiar, trailing 'tail' the like of which neither of them had ever seen.

'Whether this Eccentricity was the conscious
Intent of its Architects, or whether it be instead a
consequence of Chance and Fate, no living Man
can say.'

Pinchbrow, you fool, of course it was built this way!
Standing stones cannot be shuffled as if they were dominoes!
But why? That is the question, you old ghost… the question
you leave behind to haunt me…

The Professor read on, reaching the most tantalising passage of all.

'It is Rumour'd that the Maids once were
gather'd about a King Stone (a thing of some
Power and Virtue, believed to have Restorative
Properties of considerable magnitude), but due
process of Excavation expos'd naught but the
Loam and Clay of these Parts, upon which the

'Maids, as they are call'd, do nestle, not mov'd since the Flood.'

Standing there on that damp and stormy day, both men had been sure, in head and heart, that finding the mythical King Stone would be the key to understanding the circle and the mysterious, long-gone people who had built it.

To the Professor, this was an irresistible prize. He cared little for pounds, shillings and pence, but he longed for knowledge and for the fame that a wonderful find might bring. His first spark of interest had been fanned to a flame and then to a roaring fire of ambition. Within weeks of his first look at the book he had planned an extended summer dig in the Marches. He had confidently crowed to his University colleagues that he was about to make the most celebrated archaeological discovery of the last fifty years at least. Both actions he now regretted with all his heart.

Stones, by God! Confound you and your wretched mystery!

The Professor angrily threw the book onto the ground, where it lay dead, flopped open at the offending pages as if in one final taunt. Kicking it closed, he covered his eyes with his hands and frowned in deep and desperate thought.

It's the shape… it has to be the shape! But what in God's name is it telling us? What can it mean? How can it lead us to the King Stone… and, by God, how can I find it out when every waking moment is taken up with some trivial business of new tool-handles or enough eggs for seven or Montfalcon and his damnable dates and deadlines? And Gilbert with those endless potshards and buckles and infernal, plodding ways? There is no time! There is no time*!*

When no new thoughts came, Professor Warrington could do nothing but wearily rise from the chair to return to his task.

The only place I'm going to find that damnable King Stone is on my own head, and the weight of it crushing me to powder.

It gave him some small comfort to tread on the book as he strode off onto the site.

Tom, pausing between errands, watched him go by. He knew from bitter experience that it was pointless to try to improve his father's dark moods, so he stayed out of his way and turned his mind to happier things. He was looking forward enormously to an evening with the Gypsies. There would probably be music and maybe dancing as well as the rabbit stew, which would certainly be a hundred times better than the meal of the night before. Tinman's wife, Willow, had a way with meat and vegetables and wild herbs that bordered on magic.

I'm glad Father said we could go tonight. I hope he remembers, since he didn't even seem to be listening, as usual. I want to see Pigsticker, and ask him about that stone of Gilbert's, if he'll let me. Something about it bothers me.

"Tommy! Stand still and look at me!" a familiar girlish voice called out just behind him.

"What?" exclaimed Tom, turning at the sound.

There was Geraldine, clicking away with a camera and looking tremendously pleased with herself.

"What do you think of this, then?" she asked, doing a little twirl before holding out the camera for his approval.

"Very nice, I'm sure," said Tom flatly, to hide how impressed he really was.

The little camera was very different from the one which the Professor had borrowed from the university for the recording of the dig. The university owned old, sturdy models, which were placed on cumbersome wooden tripods – steady in all conditions, but horribly awkward to lug around. This was a far smaller and sleeker affair, complete with a shiny brown leather case.

"The very latest Kodak model, from America," stated Geraldine, "it can take a hundred pictures with one film. Expensive, of course, but Papa says *I'm worth it*."

You're worth a slap... not that you'll ever get one, of course...

"I'm sorry, Geraldine, but I'm busy," he told her, putting his hands in his pockets and striding determinedly away.

"Oh, that's all right," she trilled in response, hurrying along after him, "I want to capture the real... *essence* of what happens here, so just try to look natural... if you can. Your father says I'm welcome. You just carry on. Leave the *Art* to me."

Then, with a mocking wave, Geraldine trotted off to find a suitable point from which to take her photographs.

Where does she get her grand ideas of herself? 'Art' for heaven's sake! 'Real essence!' What does she know about anything real? Like hard work for instance? Like long hours, dust and muck, gritty eyes, carting soil about until your arms ache, and running errands in the heat until you get sunstroke? Has she ever worked on anything in her whole life?

Tom tried to ignore the camera's clicking and

whirring, which seemed to go on for most of the morning. By the looks on the faces of the students and the Professor, they weren't too happy with it either, particularly John, when Geraldine suddenly snapped him from close up as he struggled up a ladder from the bottom of the pit. He promptly dropped the basket of soil and rocks which he had been lugging under his arm. Geraldine alone found this hilarious.

Finally, to everyone's relief, Miss Montfalcon called a halt to her photography. She had taken a whole film of pictures, ignoring the expense of developing and printing. The archaeological team had no such luxury. They had been forced to be very careful and economical in making their photographic record, to save on funds, which Geraldine found highly amusing. As she prepared to leave, she charmed the Professor into telling Thomas to escort her to the road, where the driver would be waiting for her in the motor car. Tom groaned, but went along and even carried her bag. He loved to look at cars.

All the way to the road, Geraldine chattered on, fitting in several snide comments about archaeology, Gilbert, Pigsticker, and 'outdoor ablutions', which she declared to be fit only for animals. But the sight of the car, with its shining black paint and gleaming brass lamps, and the sound of its engine as it roared away, made it worth the effort. And besides, Tom was used to appearing to listen while paying no attention at all.

Later though, Tom listened with greater attention as his brother shared some of his knowledge of motor cars during the walk to the Gypsies' camp. Talking more quickly than usual in his excitement, Gilbert listed facts and figures and compared Mr Montfalcon's car with others he had seen or read about. His passion for cars matched Tom's, though Tom wondered whether Gilbert had ever imagined what twenty horsepower or seventy miles an hour would actually feel like.

The wind in your face, the steering wheel in your hands... all that power... all that speed, going anywhere you like... marvellous... If you've got two thousand pounds to buy one, of course. Father says 'motor cars are a menace to peace and quiet and if people like Mr Montfalcon have their way cars will take over, all of the countryside will be eaten up by roads and there won't be any trees or horses or grass or archaeological sites anywhere any more'... but surely that could never happen?

The sun was sinking slowly in the sky, its heat diminished, bathing the trees in a rich, amber light. A pair of chaffinches watched the boys from a low branch and, deeper in the wood, a jay chattered.

"Look, Thomas!" whispered Gilbert suddenly, stopping himself in mid-flow and putting out an arm to bring Tom to a halt.

He pointed up ahead, and there, ambling along the path not twenty feet away, was a badger. Looking at it, Tom felt half a memory brush across his mind, but it was gone before he could grasp it.

"*Meles Meles*," said Gilbert, with a half smile. It was one of the hundreds of Latin names he knew.

At this, the badger stopped and looked round. It seemed to give the boys a hard stare, then it sniffed once and trundled off into the bracken. The ferns rippled briefly, then all trace of the creature was gone.

"He didn't think much of that," Tom laughed, and the two boys carried on walking again.

Tom judged this as the moment to raise the matter of the strange stone.

"Gil," he said, then came straight to the point the way Gilbert liked. "That stone you found. I know you don't want to mention it to Father, but there's something odd about it. What about asking Pigsticker if he knows what it is, or if he's heard of anything like it?"

Gilbert was quiet for a long moment and he seemed to be thinking hard. Eventually he answered.

"At present, Thomas, I would rather that nobody knew about the stone except you and me. I cannot give you a good reason for that and I admit to being rather confused about the whole matter. But I ask you not to speak of it to anyone, at least for a while. I need more time to think about it."

And there the subject was left.

CHAPTER 5

"The Eyes says they has Her, so what now?"

What now indeed. Willow says they must have a part in the Joining, and all here knows that she Sees true. But I says, us should take Her back, and do what's fit without them.

Although Tinman did not speak the words aloud, Pigsticker plainly saw the intent in his friend's eyes. Mother Bessamy, who had asked the question, saw it as well. It matched the dearest wish of her own heart, that no outsider's hand should have a part in what was to come. But she knew that this was not how it was to be.

"If they has Her, they must bring Her – and bring Her of their own free will," said Willow quietly.

"And if they does not?" asked Tinman, his face clouded with worry.

"We must trust that they will," said Pigsticker, though he, too, looked troubled, not enjoying the taste of the words on his tongue.

"… and be ready if they won't," muttered Mother Bessamy, and her eyes met Tinman's in a look of complete understanding.

Willow looked to one side, as if hearing a sound the others could not.

"They are almost here," she stated simply, and turned to walk back to the camp.

She ushered Pigsticker and Mother Bessamy to walk before her and held out her hand to Tinman. He could do nothing but helplessly follow, entranced by her green dress sighing its way through the dry grass and by the threads of red gold in her hair.

Oh. So many people. I had not expected that. Visitors, clearly. I shall wait here for a while. I shall wait here and take sixty breaths. I shall take sixty breaths and watch for the Tinman and Willow and Rosebay and Darkus. Thomas shall wait with me and then he can lead the way. Sixty breaths. Begin. One... two... three...

From a small rise above the site of the Gypsy camp, Tom and Gilbert looked down on a scene of hectic activity. Whoever the Gypsies' visitors were, they had brought plenty of noise and colour with them. There were women in bright skirts and shawls gathering washing off the bushes where it had been spread to dry, carting water and chopping up vegetables. A group of young men and boys was building a shelter out of bent saplings and a heavy canvas sheet, directed by an old man the boys had never seen before. All the time, children and dogs ran around in a happy and unruly pack, being scolded in a mixture of English, Welsh and Romany. Smoke rose from the cooking fires and there was a general air of festival.

Who are all these people? Where did they come from?

A few extra caravans were parked at the edge of the camp. Tinman and his family owned quite plain vehicles, but these were ornamented with carving and painted in yellow, red, gold and green. Various horses were tethered nearby, cropping the grass and whisking their tails to keep the flies away. Magister, the great piebald horse who pulled the Tinman's caravan, snorted and lifted his heavy, whiskered head, for he had scented Tom, a friend who sometimes brought him a carrot in his waistcoat pocket.

"Come on, Gil" said Tom, leading the way into the camp, "we've been spotted. Let's go and say hello."

Gilbert took a final deep breath, nodded, and followed.

Tinman was splitting logs with a hatchet when he caught sight of Tom and Gilbert. He stopped his work for a moment to wave and call them over. A young man who was working alongside Tinman gave him a puzzled look.

"*Gaujos?*" he asked, just loud enough to hear.

Tom knew that this meant 'not-Gypsy'. He hoped the man wasn't unhappy that they were there.

"*Gaujos,* yes, but no trouble," Tinman replied, as Willow had taught him; "friends of ours."

As if to prove the point, Senso, the Tinman's lurcher, ambled over and sat beside Tom, thrusting his rough head under his hand for a pat.

"Good enough," the man said, and went back to chopping wood for the fire.

"Evening, Master Thomas, Mr Gilbert," said a familiar voice, and there, appearing in his sudden way, was Pigsticker.

"You is just in time for dinner," he said, and indeed, the company was beginning to drift towards the logs placed as seats around the main fire, with various plates and dishes in hand.

Pigsticker led them over to where Willow was sitting,

stirring something in a large metal pot over the fire. She smiled up at them.

"Good job you brought me those extra *shoshis*," she said to Pigsticker, "when you brings me hungry *chavos* like these to cook for!" and she pointed her spoon at Tom and Gilbert, who were both looking eagerly into the stewpot.

"Now make yourselves useful," she told the boys, "and go and bring me some *kosht*."

She motioned the boys over to where the firewood was piled up, and they went to fetch some for her, carrying the sticks back in awkward armfuls. Pigsticker sat on a log seat and filled his pipe. Soon the evening air was scented by tobacco smoke as well as the rich aroma of the stew.

The meal certainly lived up to Tom's hopes. The rabbit stew was wonderful, with chunks of succulent meat and a tasty gravy full of wild herbs and pieces of onion. As well as this, there were potatoes cooked in the edges of the fire (called '*tattitatti*') and meat roasted on spits, blackened and crisp on the outside and deliciously juicy on the inside. As they ate, Willow joked with the boys, saying that they were eating '*hotchi*', remembering how they had been shocked that a hedgehog could be thought of as food. The Gypsy children gathered round, finding Tom and Gilbert both interesting and strange. Clearly, gaujos had some peculiar ways.

The evening was darkening, and the camp was lit by the flickering light of the fires and a few flaming torches which the Tinman had made and placed around like giant candles. Plates and pots were pushed aside with satisfied sighs and extra wood was thrown onto the main camp fire, making it blaze up brightly and send a crackling shower of sparks into the sky. Those gathered around it began to look expectantly towards certain members of the company, and, with a joking show of reluctance, these few went to their caravans and returned with musical instruments; fiddles, whistles, a banjo and a drum.

Tom felt a growing excitement as the musicians tuned up and then broke into a set of jigs that got everybody clapping and tapping their feet. He loved music, and especially the fast, wild dance tunes that the Gypsies played. The old man who had directed the tent-building turned out to be a marvellous fiddler. His fingers flew so fast on the strings that they were just a blur, and his bow moved in and out just as if it had a life of its own. After each tune, those watching from the log seats round the fire clapped and whistled and called out for more.

Tom watched excitedly as, one after another, the Gypsies got up to dance on a flat square of wood put out for the purpose. Tapping and twisting, each danced in his or her own style, and took the applause of the whole group when they came to a breathless halt. Tom was pushed, half-shy, half-grinning, to take a turn himself. Tinman and Willow's daughter, Rosebay, had shown him more or less what to do and he threw himself madly into the dance, arms and legs flying, to the sound of the racing fiddles and the pounding of the drum.

Gilbert, who never danced, watched him from the sidelines and clapped along, more or less in time to the music, a faint smile on his face. When the musicians finally stopped for a break, Tom flopped down next to his brother in a grinning, panting heap, while the Gypsy youngsters laughed and clapped. Pigsticker, sitting on Gilbert's other side, watched them with a twinkle in his dark eyes.

"More spirit than skill, I'd say, eh, Mr Gilbert?" he commented.

"Definitely so," replied Gilbert seriously, then looked down at Tom and broke into a rare chuckle.

Tom put on an aggrieved face and Willow's youngest son, Cobby, reached up to pat his head to make him feel better, which made everyone laugh again.

While the musicians took a rest and refreshed themselves with a drop of beer, other performers stepped forward to entertain the company. The young man who had been cutting the wood with Tinman stood up to tell a story. Tom and Gilbert struggled to understand it, knowing only a few words of Romany, but it seemed to be a story of a fox who outwitted a clumsy hunter time after time, and always got away with a stolen chicken, a dozen eggs, or even a full roast dinner. When the fox did something clever or funny, lots of people looked over at Pigsticker, who looked puzzled and innocent every time.

The story went down very well, making the Gypsies roar with laughter and call out comments all the way through. At the end, the young man took a bow and as the listeners clapped, he held out his hand towards Pigsticker, who got up and made a small bow of his own. Tom wondered what it was all about, but it added to his admiration for the old man. There was clearly more to him than met the eye.

Then it was the turn of Tinman and Willow's twins, Rosebay and Darkus. They sang a song which was like an argument, which suited them well. It ended in both of them storming off in opposite directions, while everybody clapped and laughed and Tinman lightly cuffed them both. Then there was an exciting few minutes as one of the older boys juggled with fire-sticks, first three, then four. The watchers gasped as the burning sticks flew faster and higher, dazzlingly bright against the woodland darkness, and he caught them faultlessly every time.

Now, as the applause died away, Tom became aware that quite a few people were looking at Gilbert, and he realised that they were expecting him to offer some sort of entertainment as well. Tom nudged him and said, "Gil, do one of your poems."

Gilbert, though nervous in many situations, was good at reciting. He had learned over time to pretend that the audience wasn't there, so that he wouldn't be afraid to speak. He stood up quite willingly and, as Tinman explained briefly to everyone who he was, he closed his eyes, thinking which poem to recite. When the right one came to his mind, he spoke it clearly in Welsh, while the families all hushed to listen. It went like this:

Poni welwch-chwi'r hynt y gwynt a'r glaw?
Poni welwch-chwi'r deri'n ymdaraw?
Poni welwch-chwi'r môr yn merwinaw – 'r tir?
Poni welwch-chwi'r gwir yn ymgweiriaw?
Poni welwch-chwi'r haul yn hwylaw – 'r awyr?
Poni welwch-chwi'r sŷr wedi r'sythiaw?
Poni chredwch-chwi i Dduw, ddyniadon ynfyd?
Poni welwch-chwi'r byd wedi r'bydiaw?

As Gilbert recited, the Gypsies began to look at each other with looks on their faces that Tom couldn't read in the firelight, but the glittering of dark eyes made his skin prickle slightly under his shirt. Then, all as one, several of the adults gasped out loud. After that, they fell utterly silent, leaving Gilbert to finish alone, his words hanging heavy in the still night air.

"*Da iawn*," said Pigsticker softly, as Gilbert sat down, "you do rightly, young man, keeping words like them in your heart."

Gilbert nodded silently.

So Pigsticker knows Welsh! He doesn't sound Welsh, though. Perhaps he lived there at some time, I wonder where? Maybe he's been to Harlech, where Mother came from? I must ask him some time. Maybe he even met her...

But there was no time to ask now, for the children had quickly shaken off the strangeness of the moment and had gathered round Pigsticker, clamouring for a story.

"I don't know no stories," Pigsticker protested, shaking his head and holding his hands out as if to show that there was nothing in them.

"You do!" they shouted together, and Pigsticker quickly relented.

"Oh well," he said, his eyes glinting in the firelight, "perhaps I can just about find one rattling round in my head somewhere..."

At this, children and adults alike settled themselves to listen.

"I'll tell you a tale," (Pigsticker began) "it's a tale for this season and I'll tell it to you with rhyme and with reason.

"There was once a young king, and he ruled a fine land,
By the sense in his head and the strength in his hand,
And his words they were kind, and his judgement was fair,
Happy times for that land and the folk who lived there.

"There was fruit in the orchard, and lambs in the fold,
And the harvest of corn was as heavy as gold,
The land was alive and the people were good,
And the nightingale sang in the heart of the wood.

"Now see," said Pigsticker, interrupting his rhyme and wagging a finger at the children, "there wouldn't be much of a story if everything just went on happily like that. We needs a sad bit."

And so he continued:

"But as the years passed, and the king he grew older,
The summers got wetter, the winters came colder,
The crops they grew smaller, the people more mean,
And the land it turned greyer, where once it was green.

"The king looked to somebody older and wiser,
He asked for advice from his chiefest advisor,
'I'm lonely,' the king said, 'and tired of life.'
'What you need, my lord,' he replied, 'is a wife.'"

Pigsticker stopped himself again.

"That should be easy enough to put right," he said, "after all, a king can marry whoever he wants, can't he? But this king had been unlucky, see. When he was a lad he'd once run into a horrible witch. He'd had a bit of a fight with her, and she'd put a curse on him, that he would never ever have a wife, for no woman of flesh and blood would ever marry him. So now he was stuck, wasn't he?

"But the king had a wizard with magical powers,
Who made him a girl out of branches and flowers,
He said secret words and brought her to life,
And the king was well pleased with his beautiful wife.

"For years they were happy, they raised a fine boy,
The kingdom was known for its plenty and joy,
And the heart of the land had a strong steady beat,
You could feel it come up through the soles of your feet.

"Now," said Pigsticker in an ominous voice, "you can guess what that witch thought when she heard about that! She was in a rare old rage! She screamed so loud that she broke all the glass for miles around, and set the dogs a-howling! She wanted to punish that king in the most evil and terrible way she could think of, and let me tell you, she had some shocking nasty ideas in her head, did that one… so she flew to his kingdom and turned up in his hall, and she cursed him again, even worse this time! She said he'd lose his wife, his land would go to ruin and he wouldn't live to see his son grow up into a man. Three curses in one! That's how hateful she was.

"Now the king, he was terrified, because his wife had gone out to the woods, where she loved to go (her being made out of flowers, I expect she felt at home out there, more than in the palace), and she'd taken their boy with her, to watch her dance with her ladies at a special clearing she knew. And somehow the witch read all that from his eyes, and she flew off faster than the king could chase her, even on his very best horse.

"And sad was the end of the flower-girl queen,
Who danced with her ladies that day on the green,
The hag cast a spell with a wand made of bone,
And turned the poor queen and her ladies to stone.

"The king he rushed up on his fastest black mare,
But the stones and the silence were all he found there,
And he wept for the wife and the son that had died,
And his eyes were blind from the tears that he cried.

"He stumbled away and he let out a groan,
And there in the wood, he too turned to stone,
And a cold grey rock was all that was left,
Of a love and a curse and a king, bereft.

"Now, that would be a very sad place to end a story, would it not?" Pigsticker remarked, looking at the stricken faces of the children, just visible in the firelight. "So let me tell you the rest…

"What the king never knew was that his son had been up a tree while his mother and her friends were dancing, and he'd fallen asleep on a thick branch. The spell missed him, for you see, he never looked on the witch. But when he woke up, he was all alone and lost in the woods with his mother vanished and gone. Some say it was a fox, some say a badger, that showed him the way home. Most say he grew up to be a good king in his father's place, but everyone agrees that neither he nor any king after him could get things back to how they had been in the good old days. After the days of the king and the flower-queen, the kingdom went downhill ever after.

"But that's not the end of it! Oh, no. 'Tis said that every hundred years or so, on a special night in the summer, there's a chance for the king and the queen to be brought back together, and if they are, then the land will come alive again, and be stronger than ever. Don't know if that's true, though," Pigsticker admitted, with a shrug.

"But what about the witch? What happened to her?" Rosebay called out, and Pigsticker looked at her with a smile.

"Oh, her," he said.

"That hag's dead and gone, just dust and old bones,

But the legend lives on, and so do the stones."

And with that, Pigsticker ended his story-telling. Tinman brought him a jug of beer and he took a long drink. The old fiddler played a last, quiet melody and slowly the group began to break up as mothers gathered up their sleepy children to take them to their blankets.

"That was the right tale for these times, and well told," said Willow, nodding to Pigsticker as she carted Cobby off to his small bed in the Tinman's caravan.

Tom yawned and stretched and Gilbert took out his pocket watch.

"Fourteen minutes past ten," he stated.

"Time to be going," said Pigsticker. "I'll wander along with you; I could do with a stretch."

A few moments later, after saying goodnight and thanking everyone for the food and the welcome, Tom led the way back through the woods towards the Professor's camp. Tinman had handed Gilbert a flaming torch and they moved through the wood in its flickering light. Tom felt unusually alert and oddly excited. He was sure that, in the shadows beyond the torchlight, twigs were snapping and leaves rustling. Several times, from the corner of his eye, he thought he saw something moving among the trees. The last time, he turned quickly, wide-eyed, hoping to catch sight of whatever was moving.

Yes! A figure, almost invisible in the shadows, flitted behind a tree – there, but gone in an instant. The hair stood up on the back of Tom's neck.

"Did you see that?" he asked, breathlessly.

"No," said Pigsticker calmly, from behind them, "and nor did you."

Puzzled, Tom stopped and turned to ask him what he meant. But the old man was gone.

"Oh," said Tom, disappointed but unsurprised.

Gilbert seemed not to have noticed anything unusual and he walked on calmly, with his familiar heavy tread. After taking one last, fruitless look around, Tom gave up and ran along after him, not wanting to stray outside of the torchlight.

"Gil," he said to his brother, "that poem sounded good, though I didn't really understand it. I only got 'sea' and 'Earth' and the bit about believing in God. I don't think I'd ever heard it before. Is it a new one you've been learning?"

"It is not a new one," Gilbert replied, trudging on, "it is very old. Very old indeed. It is a poem about the end of the world, Thomas – the sea rushing over the land, the sun sailing away and the stars falling to Earth. I cannot remember when I learned it. I did not even know that I knew it, though evidently I did know it. I find that most peculiar."

Peculiar? That's more than peculiar! Gil always knows when he read or learnt anything, usually exactly, to the day. How could he know a poem and not know that he knew it? Where did it come from, how did it get into his head? That is... weird.

Tom waited for Gilbert to say more, but he remained silent. Tom knew not to press him. After a few more minutes, they came to the edge of the camp.

"Father has waited up," Gilbert observed, and there, up ahead, was the light of his lantern, warm and familiar, calling the boys back home.

CHAPTER 6

All the next day, and the one after that, Tom's strange mood never quite went away. Like a haunting phrase of music, a vague, unsettling feeling played around the edges of his mind. Mainly it was barely noticeable, but now and again, a wave of the night-time's strange, wild excitement would suddenly well up from the back of his mind, gather force, and wash over him. The silent rush would momentarily swamp all his thoughts and feelings. As it ebbed away each time, it left him slightly breathless, like a swimmer coming up from underwater and back into the light.

Between the strange waves, an odd calm would descend wherever Tom was standing. It turned the air unnaturally still and hazy and made the small sounds of bees and birdsong seem unusually clear. And through it all, there came, again and again, that feeling of being watched; of tireless eyes boring through the hot, bright sunlight or through the dim and dappled shade, always following, but never there to be seen. Several times Tom turned round suddenly, hoping to catch out the hidden watcher, but there was never anything there but empty space, trees or, once, a young blackbird, which flew away in a sudden, fluttering panic that matched that of Tom's heart exactly.

I don't know what's wrong with me. Who would be

watching me? If Father notices I'm not listening properly or says I'm daydreaming he'll get into an awful rage, and the students would just laugh. I must pull myself together. That's it. Pay attention.

So Tom went about his work on the site as he always did, but he found that he repeatedly forgot where he was supposed to be going or what he had gone to fetch. The third time that he had to go back and ask again, Arthur sighed and tutted theatrically and asked him where on Earth he'd left his memory that day.

"I can't remember," Tom replied, grinning, and quickly ducked to avoid the clod of dusty soil that Arthur lobbed at him in response.

The Professor looked on, sour-faced.

There they go again, fooling around as if this is some kind of holiday. I should go and bark at them really, but would it do any good? This is the worst dig in years. I shall be a laughing stock at the University. Old Warrington's losing his mind, they'll say, chasing after legends and fairies in the woods. And where is Gilbert? I've never known him disappear so frequently. Where does he keep going? And how can I ask when he'll just get in a state and start that dreadful groaning? Oh God, Bethan... why did you have to leave me with all this?

But there were no answers to be found, and work, for once, gave the Professor little comfort. All the while, the well-worn pain of missing his wife, gone several years and rarely mentioned, ground him down like a nagging ache in the shoulders and back.

Tom had also noted his brother's absences from the site. Like the Professor, he had been surprised to see

Gilbert breaking the rhythm of his day's work. He had taken to finding any excuse to go back to his tent, even claiming to have forgotten something, when everyone knew well that his memory was faultless.

"He's got some young lady in there," said John, winking at the other students in an exaggerated, music-hall fashion.

Tom tried to respect his brother's privacy, knowing that he never liked to be disturbed when he had chosen to be alone, but he did once happen to pop back as if by chance to his own tent while Gilbert was missing from his work. All he heard was Gilbert talking quietly in Welsh, which was nothing out of the ordinary, except that it would not usually happen during working time. Tom resolved not to pry and simply headed back to his own work, to avoid annoying the Professor. His bark might be worse than his bite, but the bark was bad enough.

On the third day after the evening with the Gypsies, the Reverend Pilcher dropped in for an unexpected visit. Arriving with a copy of the *Parish News* broadsheet for the Professor (which had proved useful as a fan on the hot walk from the village), he greeted everyone in his cordial way. He then drew his old friend into a long discussion about the stones, along with much poring over the diagrams and measurements which had been produced over the last few days. Tom, delivering drinks to the workers, caught a fragment of their conversation:

"Think about it, Ronald," the Reverend was saying, "a site like this, an ancient stone circle… it has a long, long history. It's been an important place for generations of people, meant a lot to them, in ways we may or may not be able to understand. People have come here to… reach out to something; to go away from the everyday world and into whatever lies beyond. God alone has seen all that has happened here over the centuries... who knows what stories began here, what echoes linger... and maybe, just now and then, they reach out to us, touch our mind or our soul..."

Tom would have liked to listen but didn't want to be in trouble for eavesdropping. More importantly, Gilbert was missing again and needed to be found. As Tom searched the site for him, the words went round in his head. He couldn't help but think of Pigsticker's story from the night before.

Why did he tell it all in English? There were no Romany words in it at all, not like the other stories... 'I'll tell it to you with rhyme and with reason'... was it meant for us, for me and Gil, somehow? If so... why? Should I tell Father about it? It might help with the dig... or would he just think it was nonsense and get annoyed... again?

Tom stood at the edge of the wood, wondering what to do. At once, it came again; that eerie feeling of being watched, and with it, the light prickling of goosebumps rising. He tensed, curious, wanting to turn round but hardly daring to move... then he almost jumped out of his skin, as a hand landed squarely on his shoulder.

"Oh good heavens, Thomas, I'm so sorry!" came the Reverend Pilcher's voice as Tom spun round, wide-eyed and startled. "I didn't mean to frighten you. Didn't you hear me? But you did look rather deep in thought. Are you all right? You look as if you've seen a ghost."

"I'm fine," said Tom, though his heart was still racing. "I was miles away. Sorry."

"Yes," the Reverend began, "I was just saying to your father, Thomas... being in this place can make a person feel *different* somehow; dreamy, perhaps, or more imaginative than usual... more inclined to lose oneself. My own theory is that places like this have an effect on the mind that we have yet to understand, and I believe that the stories that are told about them may be a part of it..."

"But, all those stories," said Tom, interrupting the Reverend's musings, "are they true, or just made up?"

"Come over here for a minute, Thomas," said the Reverend Pilcher in reply, indicating the main part of the excavations in the centre of the stone circle. The two of them walked across the site then stood, side by side, looking down into the pit.

"Look there," the vicar continued, "see how the layers of soil are all different, and each holds part of the long history of this place. Each one is rather like a chapter in a book – no one, on its own, tells the whole story; you need all the parts. Even then, you have to fill in some gaps with your own ideas, use your imagination. That's how it is with the stories that people tell about places like this. Fragments of fact get mixed in with bits of mystery and magic – people often use magic to explain things they don't understand, after all."

"But how could something like that affect someone's mind, Reverend Pilcher?" asked Tom, thinking of Gilbert and beginning to worry.

"Well, Thomas, think about it..." the vicar replied thoughtfully; "love and loss, magic and mystery, death and joy... all the most powerful experiences that people live through, all the things that they think and dream about, tend to be woven into their stories. And into their religion, for that matter. But true, or not true? Who can say? Possibly both. Maybe neither. I'm not being very clear, am I? And I'm forgetting my errand. Your father asked me to speak to you about Gilbert. Does he seem well to you at present?"

"Oh," said Tom, feeling slightly caught. "Erm, yes, he seems fine, but I'll keep an eye on him if Father wants me to."

"Good lad," said the Reverend, smiling briefly at Tom before turning to set off back to the village, where, he said, visits to the sick awaited him.

As his long legs carried him away from the site, the vicar set his straw hat against the glare of the sun and tried to ignore the constant slipping of his spectacles on his thin, bony nose.

A fine young man is Thomas. I just hope Ronald appreciates what he's got. And Gilbert... a most unusual person, but with such vast potential...

He made a mental note to mention all of his friend's family in the polite and private debate he would have with his God later on, at evening prayers. Then he dutifully set his mind on the afternoon's visits, working hard to remember which ailment went with each elderly parishioner.

Which will make the worst cup of tea today, I wonder? I favour Mrs Jones to take the prize, as hers is the only brew that actually has lumps in it... what an unworthy thought. Forgive me, Lord.

Reverend Pilcher stopped at the top of the fields to look around at the view which he loved. He took a moment to take off his troublesome spectacles and fan himself briefly with his hat. Then, as he turned to clamber over the stile, he felt a strong and sudden certainty that somebody was behind him, watching him go. He turned to look, expecting to see Thomas, who would probably have been sent after him with a final message from his father. Yet no one, not even a rabbit, was to be seen.

"Curious," he thought, but with no time to investigate, he left it at that.

Meanwhile, on the archaeological site, work was carrying on, but slowly and uncertainly, without clear direction. Between errands, Tom had time to wonder further about Pigsticker's tale and the unexplained events on the walk home.

Did I see someone, or did I not? And why was Pigsticker so keen to say it was nothing? What does Reverend Pilcher mean… about this place affecting your mind? Am I going mad, imagining things that aren't there? Or is there something real going on… something to do with that old story, maybe? And what's happening with Gil? I don't know, and I don't know who to ask. Pigsticker, maybe… if I can ever find him.

Tom was quite glad to be distracted from his thoughts when, later on, Father called him over and asked him to go down to the village. He was to take Mr Moss his overdue payment for mending the tools and to bring back some supplies from the grocer's shop. As ever, the students asked him to bring all kind of unlikely items: a barrel of tar, a croquet mallet, a ship's anchor, a stuffed crow – finishing up with, "Oh, and an elephant, please, if you spot a nice plump one in the baker's window," from Arthur. Tom rolled his eyes. Gilbert glanced up from the ledger, perplexed. Tom didn't even try to explain.

Gilbert thought carefully for a few moments, then gave his brother a few pennies and asked him to bring back some bullseyes, saying that Tom could share them, in return for having given him a portion of the honeycomb. Gilbert seemed to keep a tally in his head of such things, as he had ever since he was young child. He had struggled with sharing and had to be taught some rigorous rules about it, which had stuck with him as everything did. Tom quite liked it and believed that if Rosebay and Darkus had a similar arrangement, many of their squabbles might be prevented – and the Tinman might not have to box their ears quite so often.

Tom wondered what it must be like to have so many fights and quarrels. He and his brother had rarely even argued, though Gilbert had had some spectacular tantrums in his time, and many a wall in their house was dented or scarred where he had thrown things in his rages. A potted aspidistra had died a spectacular death this way, Tom particularly recalled. Luckily, nothing like this had happened for a long time.

As he strolled across the common, Tom thought about his brother and the strange stone which he had found. Gilbert had been known to get attached to a possession before and to become very bothered and worried if it was out of sight for any length of time, but this had never been a secret thing and it had always had a reason. Like in the last days before he went off to boarding school, he had been terrified and held onto his favourite fossil like a talisman that could somehow keep him safe. But he had no reason to feel frightened now, did he?

No. This is different. I'm sure all his disappearing is to do with the stone. He feels it, I feel it – something is certainly, certainly going on. Something unusual, something peculiar. I wish I had more ideas about what it could be...

Tom was so busy thinking about these matters that he barely noticed when he came to the stile and he had to walk back some way to give himself a decent run at vaulting it. This time, his foot clipped the top of it hard, sending a jolting pain up his leg. He landed awkwardly – not quite falling, but stumbling clumsily. He awarded himself a mere three out of ten and walked on, limping slightly, through the swaying barley and down to the road. Almost immediately he heard the roar of an engine from some way behind him and then the deep honking of a car horn.

"Just what I needed," he thought, as the Montfalcons' Lanchester Lagonda pulled up next to him in a cloud of dust.

"Tommy!" called Geraldine, from the back seat.

"Oh, hello, Geraldine," he replied, with forced politeness, "out for a drive?"

"It would seem so," she replied, speaking slowly and clearly, as if to an idiot. "I'm going into the village. I hear that one of your Gypsy friends has set up as a fortune teller there and I felt like having my palm read, or whatever it is they do. I'm sure it's all rubbish, but I was bored, so I borrowed the car..."

Yes, and the driver too. It was probably his afternoon off, you selfish brat.

"Are you going to the village as well?" Geraldine asked, in a slightly more pleasant tone.

"Yes," Tom replied, and he felt a moment's wild hope

that Geraldine might offer him a chance to ride in the marvellous car. But it was not to be.

"I might see you there then, unless I'm fortunate," she said, with a smile like a nettle sting.

The driver gave Tom a sympathetic look and silently mouthed, "Sorry, lad," then he put the car into gear and pulled away. Another cloud of dust rose from the dried-out road.

"Thank you very much, Geraldine," Tom said out loud, resentfully, then he added several more words which his father would have been very displeased to hear, hoping they would make him feel better. They didn't. Tom let the car and its dust get well ahead of him before snatching up a piece of wayside grass to suck on as he walked on toward the village. It tasted dull and bitter, tainted by dust and smoke, and he soon threw it away.

As he walked the last quarter-mile to the smithy, Tom couldn't help but dwell on Geraldine.

Why does she want her fortune told? As if her future could hold anything but more and more of everything she wanted, everything her family's money can buy. I wonder who the fortune teller is? I'm not sure any of the Gypsies that I know can tell fortunes… must be one of the visitors.

Tom knew that Reverend Pilcher had some unfavourable views about people interfering with God's will by meddling in fortune telling; he had warned the boys about it in quite a serious way. Father had laughed and said his sons would know better than to waste money on such nonsense. Nevertheless, Tom thought, it was a tempting idea.

Imagine seeing your own future… knowing what's

waiting for you. Riches and fame, maybe... adventures, travels... all sorts of amazing things. I will definitely go and find that fortune teller and ask her what my future holds...

But then Tom remembered, with a thud of disappointment, that he had no money of his own at all, and so the idea had to be abandoned.

CHAPTER 7

When Tom arrived at the smithy to pay the smith for the new tool handles, Mr Moss was taking a break from work, sitting outside the forge on an old water barrel and eating a huge chunk of pie that left crumbs in his beard. He noticed straight away that all was not well.

"Not like you to be down in the mouth," he said, looking down at his young friend, with his thick eyebrows drawing together in concern. "What's troubling you, Thomas?"

"Erm…" Tom began awkwardly, realising that none of his troubles were the sort that could be shared; "nothing really," he finished, with an attempt at a smile.

The smith didn't pry. He just nodded briefly, took a moment to stow the coins in a pocket stitched to his leather apron, then steered the conversation round to happier matters.

"You'll be coming to the pageant, I takes it, you and your brother?" he asked.

Tom's ears pricked up. "I haven't heard about it," he said; "what is it, and when will it be?"

"What is it? What is it?" Mr Moss replied, as if surprised that anyone wouldn't know. "It's the biggest event of the summer in these parts and only a few days away now! A bit of good old-fashioned fun, that's what it is. Games, and stalls, and dancing, morris men and folks in costumes, a few jugs of ale and a good time had by all. There'll be a play, as well, or at least, a lot of larking about on a stage… I hear the village lads are planning to ginger it up a bit, as lads will… but don't tell anyone I told you!"

Tom was beginning to be very interested indeed, and the smith had even more to tell.

"Jack Hibbert from the farm over yonder, he'll be bringing his big horse, Old Ben, for the young 'uns to have a ride on – you should hear 'em squeal when they gets up on him and sees how far away the ground is! See that shoe?" Here the smith pointed at a truly massive iron horseshoe hanging over the forge doorway. "That's one of his. Biggest I've ever made, I reckon."

"What else happens at the pageant?" Tom asked, hoping that he and Gilbert would get to go and see for themselves.

"Well," Mr Moss continued, "you might like to have a go on the test-your-strength machine; are you strong for your age, do you reckon? Me, I'm waiting to see if any grown fellow from these parts will take me on at it. I've been the champion for years though, the only one as can ring the bell, so I don't think I've much to fear there!" and he flexed his muscles to show how years of handling heavy iron had made them massive.

"What else?" asked Tom, becoming ever more interested.

"Well…" the smith went on, "there's a bit of a tradition of riddling, too; so mind you keep your wits about you! If someone asks you a riddle and you gets it wrong, there's always a chance you might get dunked in the horse trough – it's happened before!"

Tom instantly pictured Geraldine, in her pristine white dress, drenched in some stagnant, greenish, pondy-smelling water. Just as Mr Moss had intended, he began to feel considerably happier.

Geraldine's afternoon was not turning out as she had intended at all. As Tom stayed on to watch Mr Moss battle with a very spirited little grey mare who made every effort to kick off her new shoes, the heir to the Montfalcon fortune was reduced to waiting, something she truly hated. The driver had soon found the fortune teller's booth, near the village pub, but it had seemed deserted when they arrived and Geraldine's imperious call had met with no reply. Outraged, she had sent the hapless driver to search for the fortune teller and bring her back without delay.

While she waited, hot and irritated, Geraldine practised reclining elegantly on the seat of the car for a while, in a way that she had learned by watching her mother. But such style was sadly wasted on the quiet village and she soon gave it up. Tutting at the driver's slowness, Geraldine climbed down from the car and walked over to the booth again. It was a narrow, circular tent, old-fashioned and faded in places but still defiantly exotic. Its once-scarlet fabric had a few tatty spots that looked as though they had been trodden on by animals. Geraldine sniffed in distaste.

Bored and hot, Geraldine stepped into the shade of the tent. Immediately, she felt a hard tug on her skirt hem that stopped her in her tracks. Looking down for someone to snap at, she saw that the material was snagged on one of the old iron pegs that held the tent down. Snatching it off simply caused the fine material to tear and she huffed in annoyance. It was at this moment that a voice from within the tent announced, with no greeting or ceremony at all, that she had better come in.

It's about time!

Surprised, but determined not to show it, Geraldine took a moment to arrange her features into a suitably haughty look. She then pulled back the door flap by its scraggy tassel and stepped into the warm, heavy darkness of the booth. The dimness inside the tent was briefly blinding after the bright sunlight outside. A powerful scent caught in the back of Geraldine's throat – a cloying mixture of incense, tobacco, sweat and stale cakes – and she wrinkled her nose in disgust.

As her eyes adjusted to the gloom, Geraldine took in the scene inside the tent. There was a small table draped in wax-spattered cloth that might once have been velvet. On a stand beside the table a smoky lamp was burning, adding more heat than light to the small enclosed space, but throwing strange, twisting shadows onto the reddish tent walls. The lamp swung just slightly, though the air was still, making the shadows bob and dart as if they were alive. The effect was unnerving, giving the tent dark, shadowy depths, and making it feel larger, somehow, than it seemed from outside.

On a flimsy folding chair behind the table sat the fortune teller.

Just as I thought. A wrinkled old crone in a shawl. A crimson scarf, gold earrings. Let me guess, no teeth. A clay pipe, how delightful, oh, and smoke rings. If that is a trick that's supposed to impress, it hasn't worked. I think you must have read the Fortune Teller's Manual – *but only Chapter One.*

But if Geraldine had herself foreseen certain details of the fortune teller's appearance, there was something she had not bargained for. The dark, knowing eyes that looked her up and down from the elderly face threatened to shatter the poise she was putting on. Nevertheless, she spoke with her usual confidence.

"What took you so long?" Geraldine asked. "Didn't you know I was waiting?"

Instantly and rather alarmingly, the old Gypsy burst into laughter, coughing wisps of smoke from both her mouth and her nose.

"What kind of a fortune teller would I be if I didn't even know when I had a customer!" she cackled, in a high-pitched voice like that of a crow.

Geraldine looked away, thinking the woman a little cracked. She noticed a rickety wicker cage standing on the edge of the table, empty, with its floor streaky white and its door hanging off. She had just begun to wonder what kind of creature called this home when a pair of tiny, coldly gleaming eyes and a cruel black beak appeared from behind the Gypsy woman's head. Slowly, the rest of the bird followed, clambering upward, with its claws digging into the cloth of the scarf. Its head tilted sideways to stare at Geraldine, horribly interested.

Fully revealed, the creature was a magpie: moth-eaten, scruffy and long past its prime. When it turned, Geraldine could see that its tail feathers were missing, no doubt lost in some long-ago fracas, and its body ended suddenly in a clump of blackish down. But its eyes were bright, alive with intelligence and an unsettling humour. Silently, it opened its beak, revealing a stiff tongue that poked upwards like a live black grub. The bird nibbled gently at the old lady's ear and she smiled fondly at its touch.

Geraldine shuddered and stifled a gasp, wanting to leave, loathing the four piercing eyes that now locked on her and watched her intently, sizing her up. It seemed they found little to admire.

"So, girlie," the old woman said finally, and here her voice changed completely, becoming much deeper and more thoughtful; "what kind of fortune have you come seeking? Come here, my dear, and take a seat. Let's have a look at the colour of your money, and maybe I'll show you the map that fate has drawn for you."

Geraldine breathed in through tightened nostrils and stepped over to the small stool that stood beside the table. Not daring to consider how dirty it might be, she perched herself on the edge of its worn seat. Quickly and somewhat confusingly, she was talked into parting with two shillings – rather more than she had bargained for. The old lady handed the money straight to the magpie. It took it in its beak, winked at her and flapped untidily away to secrete it somewhere in the shadowy depths of the tent. When it returned, it landed on the cage and settled for a good scratch. Geraldine's skin crawled.

The Gypsy ignored her customer's distaste and reached out an affectionate hand, not unlike a bird's claw itself, to stroke her pet's dusty feathers. Then, mindful of her role, she launched into what was clearly a well-worn speech, all about fate and destiny, the mysteries of the future and the powers of the true clairvoyant.

Having expected some such nonsense – and having no intention of listening to it – Geraldine settled to looking bored. But the old lady paid no attention to her and just continued her patter without missing a word. Her customer looked heavenward and stifled a yawn, wondering how much more of scabrous birds and boring babble she would have to put up with. She had come to hear about only one thing – that is, herself: Geraldine Edwina Margaret Montfalcon.

Finally, the old Gypsy reached for Geraldine's hand and held it, palm uppermost, in her own worn fingers. Geraldine recalled the old claw touching the filthy bird and reminded herself to scrub her hands with carbolic soap when she got home. The Gypsy took her time studying the palm in the unreliable light of the lamp, tracing a yellowed finger over the lines and the small hills and plains, and humming to herself in a creaky, tuneless undertone. Finally, Geraldine ran out of patience.

"Oh, for heaven's sake!" she exclaimed. "Do you see anything, or don't you?"

The Gypsy slowly raised her head and looked straight into the girl's insolent green eyes for several moments. When she spoke, her voice was deep and steady.

"And if I do, do you think you could understand it, my girl?"

"I'm not stupid!" Geraldine snapped back, with an indignant look and a flick of her long red hair.

The Gypsy ignored her customer's tone and simply stopped to stare hard at her for a very long moment. Then she looked back down at Geraldine's palm, and made her rather ominous reply.

"Then let me just say to you, young lady, that this hand tells me that you will take a long journey – a long, hard, troublesome journey – and at the end of it, you will be nowhere but where you should have been all along."

Geraldine stared straight back at the old Gypsy for a moment, her face frosty.

"I think," she said, "that I paid for rather more than that, don't you?"

"The lady wants more, she says!" the Gypsy crowed, falling back into her old-crone voice again, but now with a sharp edge of sarcasm in it. "So what shall we give her, eh, my darling?"

She didn't seem to be addressing either her customer or the magpie and Geraldine wondered again whether she was really quite all there. Then, suddenly, the table rocked sharply, as a rough, hairy dog face thrust itself out from under the drapes. Mouth open, it panted its hot, sticky breath into the stagnant air. Geraldine hurriedly drew away from it. When it saw who was sitting there, the shaggy little terrier whined and retreated back under the table.

Geraldine merely tutted, her face like that of a cat sniffing vinegar.

Really, I can say with certainty that this is the most revolting experience of my entire life. Whatever was I thinking of, coming here?

Meanwhile, the fortune teller was reaching down under the table, bending remarkably well for her age. Using both hands, she reached under the drapes and slowly drew out a scuffed black velvet bag, held tightly closed by a drawstring. She eased the cords loose and, reaching inside, pulled out a curious object. It looked rather like a picture frame, but instead of a picture it held only an empty surface, strangely curved inwards, dark and light like the sea at night glimmering under the moon. The surface was oddly blank, as if it somehow chose not to reflect the light of the lamp which hung so close to it.

Drawing out the moment of suspense, the old lady used the bag to dust the carved, scratched frame and then laid the strange mirror carefully on the table in front of her. The magpie hopped down from the top of the cage and stood on the edge of the mirror, alternately preening and staring at Geraldine. The fortune teller put aside her pipe, and looked at her customer, most seriously.

"Scrying," she announced, "is an ancient art, known to few, and not without danger. Would you dare to look at what your future holds?"

"Of course I would," Geraldine replied immediately.

Why else would I come to a fortune teller? Foolish old woman.

"Then be silent," the old woman continued, in her deep, serious voice, "and look deeply into the mirror. Wait, be still, keep your mind from wandering, and we shall see what we shall see."

And so, both Geraldine and the old Gypsy settled to looking intently into the strange black surface, while the magpie peered silently downwards too. For a long time the mirror remained stubbornly blank. Gazing into it, the old woman became so still and her face took on such an empty look that it seemed she was barely present in the tent at all. Geraldine, also staring at the inky blackness, began to get an uncomfortable feeling that she might not be able to look away if she tried. The hot, close air itself seemed to be taut and expectant, like a breath drawn in but not released; waiting, waiting, waiting…

Finally, just as Geraldine began to want to give up, she stared hard for one last time at the surface of the mirror and noticed with a small shock that it had started to change. The coal-black surface began to look slightly but undeniably lighter. Then the surface started to quiver and shimmer, faintly at first, and it seemed that the light was coming from inside of the mirror; a greyish, blurry glow that grew and grew in the slight curve of the black glass. After a few seconds, an image was just discernible to any eye that looked very hard.

Geraldine pored over the mirror eagerly, trying to make out the details of the emerging picture. Little by little, her expression changed, until the eagerness was wiped away, and replaced by a mixture of confusion and disappointment.

"What is *that*?" Geraldine asked, her voice sudden and harsh against the thick silence that filled the tent.

Instantly the picture flickered and died, leaving the mirror blank and inscrutable once again. The magpie screeched alarmingly then let out a sudden stream of loud, harsh chattering that sounded shockingly like rapid gunfire. The dog barked sharply from under the table, and at once the Gypsy woman's eyes flashed back into life. Her customer glared as she spoke.

"If you're going to try to tell me that *that* was my future, then you must be as mad as you look!"

"What did you see?" the old Gypsy asked, steadily, undaunted by the insulting words.

"How should I know?" Geraldine flared in return, standing up to leave. "It looked like some made-up nonsense – a man, but with a badger's head, or something like that! What absolute rubbish! That thing's just a trick, a cheat, it's some kind of magic lantern, and that's all it is. What an utter waste of time and money!"

Having said her piece, Geraldine drew herself up to her full height, turned, and flounced out into the sun without a backward glance. She jerked the door flap roughly as she passed, leaving the tassel swinging wildly and dust motes swirling in the shaft of bright sunlight that she had let in.

The Gypsy woman sat for a few seconds, wide-eyed with surprise. Then she reached down to rub the whimpering terrier's ears and she spoke to him in a quiet, wondering voice.

"So, my dear, she did see it – it wasn't just me. Her, of all people! Even I didn't see that coming."

Then she turned to the magpie, which sat in a heap like a worn-out duster on the edge of the table, its eyelids flicking in tiny, leathery twitches.

"But why?" she said to it. "Why would one of Them come to someone like her? That's what I'd like to know."

The bird gave no answer, and the old lady was left to draw her own conclusion.

"Well," she said, finally, "I don't know what to make of it. But it must mean she has some part to play, as if them other gaujos wasn't enough. I'll have to tell the others – maybe they can make head or tail of it."

Then she gathered up her things and hurried out of the tent, one pet hopping and flapping alongside her, the other scurrying behind, the message being far too important to wait.

Meanwhile, out in the sun, Geraldine was still so annoyed that she had stormed off rather farther than she might have intended; she had passed by the waiting car and she was now halfway up the main street, still muttering angrily to herself. When Tom happened by, laden with supplies to lug back to the site, she didn't even bother to insult him, but launched straight into complaint.

"That fortune teller is an absolute charlatan!" she spat. "Don't waste your money on her. She just talks a lot of old rubbish and does some stupid tricks with a mirror. Complete nonsense!"

Then she flounced away, holding on to her dignity in spite of her torn and ragged skirt.

With no chance to comment, Tom watched her stomp back to the car, calling for the driver to take her home immediately. At this, Tom couldn't help but smile. He had called into the pub to buy some ginger beer, and knew that the driver was in there right now, enjoying a pint or two with his friend the publican and looking as if he was in no hurry to leave. Somehow, this made the box of groceries seem rather lighter, and Tom set off home quite happily, whistling as he went.

CHAPTER 8

Hours later, with dinner over and done and the campfire flickering away, Tom told Gilbert the story of Geraldine's terrible afternoon. Gilbert laughed his rather jerky, snorting laugh, and asked Tom to repeat it twice so he could savour every detail. Even when the Professor overheard and lectured them both sternly about the evils of enjoying another's misfortune, they struggled to hold back their smirks. Clearly believing that a little improving was called for, the Professor set Gilbert the task of reading aloud to the company from the vicar's parish broadsheet. Tom inwardly groaned.

The main item was Reverend Pilcher's own writing and his subject was the summer pageant. Tom had told his father what Mr Moss had said about it and the Professor had said neither yes nor no to going along. The vicar's article stated that these days, the pageant was held as a celebration of Lord Nelson's victory over Napoleon at the Battle of the Nile in 1798. As Gilbert dutifully read the rather dull words, Tom soon felt his attention beginning to wander. He was almost used to the feeling of eyes watching him from nearby and hardly surprised to sense them once again.

Over there! On the left... under that bush, there's definitely someone there... or something. Better not let Father catch me looking, or he'll ask me some boring question about the Battle of the Nile, but I'm sure I saw eyes...

Tom slowly peered around to the far left, straining to look beyond the light of the lamp and into the deep, dark shadows beyond. Yes! There! Low down, through the leaves, two eyes flashed red as the fire briefly flared. They stared straight at Tom for an instant, and between them, a dim white flash showed for a second, then faded back into the gloom.

Badger!

A badger, so close? That's most odd. They never come near the fire.

With a rustle and a snuffle, the badger turned and melted away into the darkness. Tom wrenched his attention back to the vicar's broadsheet. Aware that his father might quiz him at any second, he tried to pick the facts out of Gilbert's droning reading. He had moved on to a story of the parish church's own saint, St Edith.

Saxon girl… wanted to be a Christian… not allowed… village elders wanted to kill her… took her to the woods… she called on God… God turned them to stone. Wait! That's nonsense. That's not how stone circles came to be…

Tom barely heard the rest of the reading, which was just Reverend Pilcher describing how the villagers had celebrated over time. What used to be a religious procession and Mass in memory of St Edith was now a mixture of games and revelry and an irreverent pantomime. Still, the Reverend concluded, whatever form the summer pageant might take, it was a tradition that the village was pleased to keep alive and should, by the grace of God, enjoy.

"Hmm," said the Professor, as Gilbert handed the broadsheet back to him. "I suspect that the main tradition being kept alive in this case is getting riotously drunk and making enough noise to be heard across the Welsh border."

Not that that's always such a bad thing... heaven knows, Pilchard and I have downed some ale in our time, aye, and paid for it the next morning too...

Gilbert was frowning hard. When he spoke, his voice had a wavering, tearful edge that Tom recognised all too well. He crossed his fingers tightly, hoping that his brother was not about to have one of his outbursts.

"Father..." Gilbert began, "why has the Reverend Pilcher written about the stones as if they are a Christian monument, when they date back very much further than that? He knows they are Pre-Christian, he said so himself."

"Ah, well, yes, Gilbert, there is something you have to understand here," Professor Warrington began to explain. "The good Reverend has others to consider when he writes his words of wisdom. His congregation would be most upset to hear their vicar cast out their traditional story in favour of a vague pre-Christian version which we cannot even verify. No, in writing about the stones as he has, old Pilcher may have put aside historical accuracy, but he has kept his flock happy."

"But that's not right!" Gilbert protested, his tone rising in intensity and outrage. "You cannot change the truth. It is the *truth*, it is a *fact*. You have to be honest! It's important!"

Tom sensed an oncoming storm in his brother's mood. The Professor seemed oblivious.

"Not everybody can accept the truth, in every instance, Gilbert," he stated in his detached way. "Sometimes it has to be kept from them for their own sake. Just trust me, it does."

"But how can you trust anything, if people are not telling the truth?" Gilbert replied, beginning to rock to and fro. "I don't know why anyone would do that... why they would hide the facts and put lies in their place!"

He was becoming increasingly agitated and he looked downwards and breathed heavily, avoiding the eyes of his father and brother.

"But, Gil, people hide the truth for all kinds of reasons," Tom said, gently.

Like you, not telling Father about that weird stone, and not writing it in the catalogue. That's not exactly being honest, is it?

"It's a fine night for a walk," the Professor announced firmly, cutting short the discussion. "Why don't you two go for a wander. Once you get clear of the trees, there should be a fine view of the stars."

"The stars," Gilbert repeated, flatly.

Tom was a little surprised. Gilbert hadn't done what the family called his 'echo' for a long time, though he had done it a lot when he was younger. He would copy the last few words of whatever had been said to him, sometimes saying them more than once. It disconcerted strangers, who sometimes thought he was mocking them. It was another thing that Gilbert tended to do when times were difficult for him, or when he was worried.

Scrambling up, Tom said in a determinedly cheerful tone. "Yes, let's go for a walk, Gil. We can say hello to Orion."

Normally, at this kind of opening, Gilbert would have pointed out that this was a futile thing to do, as Orion was both thousands of miles away and clearly lacking ears. But this time, he simply nodded and stood up to go with his brother. But then, instead of walking straight out along the path, he turned towards his tent.

"I have to get... my coat," he explained, as he ducked through the flap.

He soon came out, with his jacket over his arm, though the night was easily warm enough to do without.

"I saw that badger again, just now," Tom told his brother as they walked along. "It was watching us from the bushes, I'd swear it was."

"It may not be the same one as we saw on the path," Gilbert said, and Tom was pleased to hear him returning to his usual tone. "But then again, it may be," he continued, "because it does seem to be an unusually fearless, inquisitive specimen. I believe that I have seen it myself on four occasions since we first came upon it on the path. I have to agree with you, Thomas, it does appear to be watching. For what reason, I do not know."

"I could ask Pigsticker," Tom suggested, "he might have some idea."

"Yes, Pigsticker does have a great deal of knowledge about the ways of wild creatures," Gilbert agreed, "even if he does call them by the most peculiar names."

Tom smiled at this. Pigsticker's country names – pishoms for bees, Arrywiggles for earwigs – were probably no stranger than Gilbert's Latin ones would sound to him.

Walking on through the still night air, trying to avoid the nettles and brambles in the dark, the brothers soon emerged from the edge of the wood. Here, as long as you avoided the rabbit droppings, the springy grass provided a fine carpet to lie on and gaze up into the endless sky.

Stretched out with his hands comfortably linked behind his head, Tom stared at a sky like dark blue velvet, with tiny diamonds scattered randomly all across it.

Gilbert saw nothing random about the sky, only the orderly constellations that he loved. He began to name them all as if reading from a book:

"Ursa Minor, the Little Bear with Polaris the North Star, and then down to Ursa Major, the Great Bear, with Dubhe, Alioth, Alcor, Alkaid, Mizar, Phad, and Merak. Then Leo, with Algieba, Denebola and Regulus..."

Tom savoured the exotic words, Gilbert's chanting tone turning them into a wizard's spell.

"You must have a star map in your head," he remarked, amazed as ever by his brother's brain.

But there came no answer, and when Tom turned his head to look over at him a moment or two later, Gilbert was no longer staring at the heavens. Instead, he was sitting hunched over, intent, and Tom saw that once again, the strange stone was in his hands.

How did he sneak that out of the camp? Fetch his coat, indeed! He was never so tricksy before...

"Gil, what are you doing?" he asked his brother eventually, but gently, so as not to startle him.

There was no reply. Gilbert continued to cradle the stone in his cupped hands, looking down at it. When he finally spoke, it was in Welsh, in the soft tone which he had used before in its presence. Tom could only just hear the words and he couldn't tell what the sentence meant, even when Gilbert repeated it, once, then twice, then over again, in a gentle murmur totally unlike the flat, empty sound of his 'echo'. Watching him, Tom felt a faint chill of unease, and it grew and grew as the seconds passed, until finally he had to voice it.

"Gilbert!" he said sharply. "What's going on?"

At this, Gilbert dropped the stone and looked up quickly, startled. His eyes were wide in the darkness, reflecting the starlight in two points of whiteness.

"Gil", said Tom, more gently this time, "are you all right?"

"I don't know what she wants," Gilbert replied, obscurely, looking past Tom, with his voice sounding muffled and strained, "and until I do, nothing will be right."

What does that mean? What 'she'? Who's he talking about? Surely not Geraldine?

But as Tom opened his mouth to speak, Gilbert struggled to his feet, still holding the stone in both hands, and started to trudge back towards the camp, the stars forgotten. Tom scrambled up and soon caught up with him, but Gilbert didn't respond to his anxious questions, just walked on, staring ahead, with his jacket once again draped over the stone.

When they arrived back, Tom saw that the Professor had retired to his tent and turned his lamp down low. Gilbert barely looked round to nod to Tom before stepping into his own tent and lacing the flap firmly closed. Even the students' tent, unusually, was dark and quiet.

So what do I do now? Something's wrong. I've never seen Gil acting like this. Should I tell Father? But I promised I wouldn't say anything... I can't do that, but I can't just do nothing. What if he's not well? I hate to think it, but what if he's... losing his mind? He's so different when he's got that stone, he's just not like himself at all. Oh, this is awful, just awful. What should I do?

But there was nothing that Tom could do at that moment except head for bed, and so he did, though sleep was very far from his mind. He watched as a white moth flew crazed rings around his lit candle, until he could bear it no longer and shooed it out into the night. But as he lay down, he felt wide awake and thoughts whirled around in his head, whirring like the moth's wings in its dangerous flight. The knotted ropes that held his mattress creaked and groaned as he moved restlessly, his body as unsettled as his mind. An owl hooted in the wood, its drawn-out cry plaintive and ghostly.

Suddenly Tom felt small and lonely, as if he were the only person left in the world. Something rustled and snorted faintly outside his tent and he tensed, for once nervous about the world beyond the canvas walls. Telling himself firmly that it was just a fox, or maybe that badger again, Tom pulled his blanket tightly around his ears to shut out the sounds. He lay with his eyes closed, determinedly pretending to sleep. Maybe, if he pretended well enough, he would wake to find that the night had passed.

He was standing in the wood again, surrounded by the mighty oaks. The cool air of the night gently touched his warm skin and mist swirled around his legs as he stood staring up into the tangle of branches. The earth pulsed slightly under his bare feet and the air hummed with a sound like the distant swarming of bees. He felt himself drawn slowly onwards, as if by the force of a magnet, moving smoothly through the trees on light feet. The leaves whispered, a tiny sound, like a sleeper's breath. Here and there a small creature darted across his path with a sudden furtive rustle, and the owl's call echoed back and forth among the trees.

Having drifted onward for several minutes, (or was it hours?) he came at last to a clearing. A mass of stars shone like silver filigree against the deep, dark blue of the night sky and the orange moon hung overhead, resting lightly among the leafy fingertips of the trees. The hairs on the back of Tom's neck began to prickle and beads of sweat formed on his forehead. For suddenly, standing still and expectant in the eerily quiet clearing, he knew, with frightening certainty, that he was not alone.

Tom froze. Tense, he held his breath.; The air around him began to feel quite different, to tighten somehow, pressing in on his chest, quivering and thrumming with suppressed excitement. Barely daring to move his eyes, he peered gingerly into the dark shadows beneath the trees. At first, he saw only the swirling of the mist, but then, once again, the wisps gathered and thickened and gained substance, until, with widening eyes, he saw several greyish figures forming in the gloom. They stood as still as stones among the trees.

Panic rose from Tom's stomach but his throat closed, keeping him from screaming out loud. Unable to turn or run away, he stood staring at the ghostly figures. As the moments passed and the mist rolled and curled away, they became more solid, more substantial, more real. Were they human? Or animal? Tom couldn't tell, the figures being shadowed against the background of mighty trees. He caught glimpses of shaded faces, of black hair, strong limbs, grey fur. Teeth that glinted in the moonlight; dark, shining eyes.

Suddenly, a deep, strong voice rang out. Tom's heart leapt, his hands clenched hard and his jaw strained against rising terror. The voice was human but the syllables were strange; impossible to understand, though oddly familiar. The words ran together in a stream, harsh yet lilting, powerful and resonant, silencing the small sounds of the night. They came from the figure directly ahead of Tom, half-hidden in the shadows, but echoed around the clearing as if spoken in chorus from all directions.

Tom's mind reeled with the force of the unknown words and the emotion that welled up through them. Fear grew like rising pressure in his chest and head, and he began to feel that he would surely pass out at any moment...

But just as he thought he could stand no more, dimly, through the muffled thudding of his own racing pulse, Tom began to hear something he could recognise; something to hold onto and maybe understand. Although the unknown speaker's language was still foreign to him, it began, haltingly, to find a place somewhere in his mind. Shreds of meaning emerged from the stream of unfamiliar words, like pictures once seen in a gallery or scraps of poetry, half-remembered.

Time lurched and stalled as Tom stood, trying hard to hold onto the words and the images they brought with them. Somewhere behind his eyes he caught a glimpse of a woman, her face streaked with tears. A wave of loss and longing washed over him; hers, or his, he wasn't sure. He saw bright stars, sweeping across the sky like rain, trailing golden threads behind them. A pattern of red and green flashed on his eyelids as if he had been staring at the sun. A strange, jagged pattern – one he knew all too well. It was the Nine Maidens, the ring stones.

"Bring them together, let them be one," sighed a whispering breath, close to Tom's ear.

He started and spun around, but could see no sign of the speaker. Still the soft undertone spoke into his mind.

"The finding is done, the finder must come."

"Let none stand between them."

"The time is coming; let them be one."

Then, suddenly, a sound like the rushing of a strong wind drowned the voices and sucked them away into empty silence, leaving their meaning hanging in the air. A split second later, blackness swallowed the scene.

Tom's eyes fluttered open, meeting only the darkness of midnight. Through his quickened breath and a faint, buzzing headache, he could still hear the odd phrases sounding in his head and his sleepy brain struggled to hold onto them. Finder and found, bring them together, take her home…

"I don't know who she is," he murmured, still caught up in the feeling of the dream.

But his body's tiredness held him down and, before he could think on it any more, he was sliding back into sleep, into a soft, warm place, out of the reach of sound and sight and reason.

CHAPTER 9

"**M**ind your step, Tom!" called Arthur, as Tom almost stumbled over the frying pan, which was spitting away on the camping stove. "That's a priceless find, you know. Romano-British, circa 250AD. Your dad dug it up ten years ago. Genuine dents from centuries of use, but still good for many a rasher."

"What?" asked Tom, whose thoughts were still scattered from the night.

Seeing his blank look, Arthur was concerned.

"Is everything all right?" he asked. "You look like you lost a guinea and found sixpence."

"I'm all right," said Tom, with an attempt at a smile. "I just had a strange dream, that's all."

"Ah!" exclaimed Arthur. "Ze funny dream! Zere is only von cure, and zat is… ze fried egg!"

Tom recognised the character – Arthur often played it; a batty doctor with a foreign, maybe Swiss, accent. He fished an egg out of the pan and slid it onto a metal plate, adding a couple of pieces of rather burnt bacon. Tom thanked him but couldn't quite find the will to play along. Arthur shrugged, crestfallen.

Chewing at the tough bacon, Tom looked around for Gilbert. He was usually punctual for all meals, but seemed to be late this morning. Wilfred, the quietest of the student workers, wandered by to snaffle an extra bit of bread, and noticed Tom looking towards Gilbert's tent.

"If you're looking for your brother, he's gone off into the wood," he said, "about half an hour since. I suppose he felt like being on his own for a bit."

Wilfred, like all the workers, was growing used to Gilbert disappearing from the site.

"Mmm, that's probably it. Thanks, Wilf," replied Tom.

But however Tom tried to hide it and carry on as normal, the last night's worry still gnawed away at him. He fretted for a chance to talk to his brother. He longed to tell him about the dream and the strange and powerful feelings which it had brought.

Gilbert arrived back on the site within half an hour, barely late enough to put an edge on the Professor's morning temper, but even so, Tom could find no chance to talk to him. First, the Professor whisked Gilbert and the ledger away to the main tent. Tom, losing on the toss of a coin, got landed with the task of hauling water from the dwindling stream. Worse, he then had to wash greasy, eggy mess off the frying pan and tin plates with a makeshift scourer made of twigs. Then there were all the oil lamps to clean and fill and finally, a letter to take to the village post office. It was a report on the progress of the dig for the University, and the Professor's face was stony as he handed over the flimsy envelope.

Arriving back from the village, hot and sticky in the midday sun, Tom's heart sank. A familiar red-maned figure was sitting in splendour on the Professor's old camp chair, in the shade of a tree. She was fanning herself with her pale straw sunhat and chatting to the Professor, who was looking around desperately like an animal in a trap. Spotting his younger son approaching, he found his escape.

"Ah, Thomas, you're back!" he called. "Excellent! Here's Miss Montfalcon come to see you, isn't that nice?"

Then he beat a hasty retreat, returning gratefully to work, leaving Tom to cope alone with the troubling female company.

"Yes, isn't that nice," repeated Geraldine, her too-pink mouth turning up in a feline smile.

"Delightful," said Tom, dolefully.

"So," Geraldine began, steepling her fingers elegantly and speaking like a school mistress, "I wonder what is afflicting dear Giddy Gilbert today? He appears to be returning to his tent rather frequently, neglecting his work quite shamefully."

And what would you know about work? Have you ever done any? In your whole life?

"You would almost think," she continued, "that he had something on his mind – if he has one, of course."

The words were skilfully aimed and they hit their target. Tom felt his face grow hot and his hands form fists, which he jammed into his pockets. The reaction was not lost on Geraldine. She smiled and raised one arching eyebrow.

"Now, now, Tommy," she said.

It was unfortunate that Gilbert chose this moment to walk through the camp. He was too preoccupied to notice Geraldine in time to avoid her.

"Well!" she exclaimed, stopping him in his tracks. "If it isn't Gilbert the filbert, colonel of the nuts!"

Geraldine had got this title from a music-hall song

which she had heard one of her servants sing, and it delighted her to taunt Gilbert with it. Now a telltale frown was on his face and Tom knew that he was already uncomfortable.

"How many bits of broken pot have you found today, colonel? Do they all fit together? How can you tell whether they make a cider jar or a hot-water bottle?"

Gilbert, still trying to answer the first question, began to look pained and his mouth opened and closed without any clear words coming out. Jubilant, Geraldine kept up her stream of inquiries, all pointless, which reduced Gilbert to a state of increasing panic. Eventually he could stand no more.

"Stop… it!" Gilbert groaned, putting his head down and pressing his bent arms tightly against the sides of his face, covering his ears to shut out the barrage of mocking questions.

Oh, no, Gil, don't! That'll just make her do it more… Gil, stay calm, don't let her do this to you…

"That's enough!" Tom snapped at her, trying to shepherd Gilbert away, without touching him, which was bound to upset him further.

"You're not funny, you know," he threw over his shoulder, "you're just mean!"

"Ooh, Tommy, I never knew you had it in you!" exclaimed Geraldine, bursting into peals of laughter.

Tom drew Gilbert away to the safety of the tent where the finds were stored. Geraldine remained where she was and anybody watching would have believed that she was laughing at the lame, churchy jokes in the parish broadsheet, which she had found beside her chair. To

Tom's relief, when he peered out of the tent a few minutes later, she was nowhere to be seen.

Thank you very much, Geraldine! I've waited all morning for a moment with Gil, to tell him about that dream, and now he's too upset to talk. What a treasure you are. Please do everyone a favour and don't come back. Ever.

Tom stayed to watch over Gilbert as he slowly calmed down. Finally, he reached for the box of index cards and quietly began to check his cross-referencing and Tom felt that he could safely leave him and emerge from the tent. Then, summoning his courage, he went and found the Professor and asked for leave to spend an hour away from the site. He agreed so easily that Tom wondered whether he had heard the question at all.

After checking that Geraldine was not following, Tom walked away purposefully, taking the path where he and Gilbert had first seen the badger. He made his way through the warm, shady wood towards the Gypsy encampment. He had decided to try to find Pigsticker and ask him about Gilbert's strange stone, though he didn't know how he would ask about it without breaking his promise of secrecy to Gilbert. As he hurried along, Tom crossed his fingers so tightly that the knuckles turned bright white.

Please be there, please be there, please be there...

At the Gypsy camp, news arrived, carried silently on the breeze.

Ah, he comes, the young one. To bring word of Her... or not? We shall see.

Twice, on the way to the camp, Tom had reason to be glad that Geraldine had not followed to watch him. The first time, a false shortcut led him straight into a low overhanging branch and he ducked too late and not low enough. The blow to the head made him gasp in pain and left a tender lump under a green streak of moss and mould in his hair. Still thinking of how to word his questions to Pigsticker, he tripped over a tree root and stumbled into a patch of nettles. He arrived in the camp dishevelled and winded, with a sore head and one hand covered in itching, burning stings.

The camp was quiet, with Pigsticker nowhere to be seen. Only Willow was visible, sitting on a log, industriously braiding corn stalks and singing to herself. Looking up as he called out to her, she immediately noted his sorry state.

"*Dordi, dordi!*" she exclaimed. "What happened to you?"

"It's nothing, I just tripped over," Tom replied.

Willow sat him down and examined the rising bump on his head and tutted with sympathy over the white rash on his hand.

"Wait you there," she said to him, "while I brings you something for the stings."

She gathered her skirts and stepped up into her caravan, moving quietly so as not to wake the sleeping Cobby. When she returned, she held a pot of green salve in her hand. Sitting beside Tom, she gently took his hand and rubbed some of the stuff lightly onto the sore, prickling skin. It had a fresh, clean scent, like wild mint, and it soothed the burning within moments. Tom looked up gratefully at Willow and for a moment he was powerfully reminded of his mother, though in truth he barely remembered her.

"So," Willow said, in her calm voice, "you can see he's not here. Can I be helping you at all?"

"Err, um… I don't know," said Tom, caught off guard and suddenly unsure of himself. "I just wanted to ask Pigsticker something, but I suppose I didn't really think I'd find him anyway."

Willow laughed lightly at this, deepening the creases around her clear, hazel eyes.

"He don't often be where he's wanted," she said, with a rueful look, "though he's mostly where he's needed."

Seeing Tom's puzzled look, Willow explained.

"He went with Mother Bessamy a day-two back," she said, "that's Tinman's *púridaia*, his grandmother. She'd been off doing the *dukkering* like she does sometimes, (you'd call that fortune telling, she explained, seeing Tom look perplexed again), and she came back all hurried and took him off somewheres. They'll be back by and by."

"Oh," said Tom, disappointed. He looked around the quiet site. "Where's everyone else gone?" he asked, never having seen the place so devoid of company.

"They're roundabout the place," answered Willow, "making ready for the festival – it being the time of the year for it."

"Oh, the pageant in the village," Tom said. "I've heard a bit about that. It's tomorrow, isn't it? It sounds like fun, but I don't know whether Father will let us go."

"Well," said Willow, carefully, "the village do have its festival. We has ours, they has theirs."

She shrugged, smiling, then looked inquiringly at Tom and asked her usual question.

"*Si tut bocklo?*"

Tom knew that this meant 'Are you hungry?' Before he could even answer her, Willow had gone to bring him some food. He happily accepted a warm hunk of brown bread, thickly spread with butter and honey.

"*Pishomgudlo*," he said, remembering the Romany word for honey from last time he had been in the camp, and Willow smiled.

Then, between big bites, Tom asked her to tell him more about the festival and how it differed from the villagers' pageant.

"Hmm," she said, considering, "some things is the same, some's different. Like, they goes by the calendar, the one writ down on paper. We goes by the summer's own time. You can't hurry the sky, see, nor tell the seasons when to come. And you has to know the what and the why of it, or the games is just games, do you see?"

"Not really," said Tom, furrowing his brow though it made the scrape on his head hurt more. He chewed the delicious bread, then asked Willow what happened at the Gypsy festival.

But Willow clearly felt that she had said enough.

"We do what's needful," she replied, giving nothing away.

Then, seeing Tom's disappointment, she said, 'But I'll tell you this; good food is a part of it; and a brew of barley beer. So's stories. And riddles – we always has plenty of riddles. Here, I'll give you one to try. What breaks when you say it?"

"What breaks when you say what?" asked Tom, confused.

"That's the riddle," Willow explained. "What breaks when you say it?"

Tom worked the question through his mind for a few moments, but no inspiration came.

"I've no idea," he admitted.

"Think on it," Willow told him, "and by the time you works it out, most likely old Pigsticker'll have found you, if he hasn't before."

Then, she got up and, with a final gentle check that Tom's head wasn't too badly broken, she returned to her weaving and singing. Tom thanked her politely for the bread and honey and the salve, then said goodbye and headed back to the site, his hour being almost spent.

So he says nothing. But they has Her, that I knows.

Willow frowned slightly over her weaving. Perhaps the others were right, after all. She hoped not.

Later, as the evening shadows began to lengthen and work on the dig gave way to cooking and chatting and resting, Tom finally took his chance to talk with Gilbert. He had found his brother sitting on the log where he himself had sat with Pigsticker, several days before. Gilbert was watching a bee, which was resting on the log next to him, its wings faintly vibrating and its antennae waving to and fro in tiny searching movements. Tom was careful not to sit on it as he settled next to Gilbert. He waited a while for him to look up, then began.

"Gil," he said, "I had the strangest dream last night. I was in the wood, and there were people there, they appeared out of the mist, and one of them was talking – I didn't know the language, but it sounded almost like some kind of…"

"Welsh," Gilbert finished for him. "Yes, I think you are right, Thomas, to note the Welsh or Celtic nature of the language. However, there were marked differences from the Welsh in use today. Possibly it was a regional dialect, a forerunner of…"

What! How could he know what I was going to say?

Tom held up his hand to cut him off in mid-sentence.

"Gilbert!" he exclaimed, "how did you know what was in my dream, what it sounded like?"

Gilbert looked at his brother, his face impassive.

"I know because I heard it," he replied, "otherwise I would have no way of knowing what you are talking about."

"But, Gil, that's impossible!" Tom burst out, "you can't have had the same dream! It's just… not possible!"

He was on his feet now, staring at his brother, wide-eyed and agitated.

"Thomas, think logically," Gilbert said, his voice calm and controlled, "consider the evidence. Tell me more about the dream."

So, taking a deep breath, Tom described, as well as he could, the echoing voices, the shadowy figures, the confusing images and sad, longing feelings and the odd, poetic phrases that he had heard, or as much of them as he could remember.

"That is interesting," Gilbert commented, when Tom had run out of words. "My own experience is both similar and different. Firstly, I saw no stars or weeping lady, though I did see the figures among the trees and also that curious badger. The voice that I heard was quite clear, and I was able to pick out most of the words, though not all were familiar. There was a word which sounded like '*brenhines*' which means 'queen', but I could not be certain of it. There were several mentions of something like '*bendigaid*', which means 'blessed'. I heard the word '*deigryn*' which means 'tear', but it could have been '*deincryd*', though it is unlikely, as that means 'chattering teeth'…"

"But Gil!" Thomas said urgently, stopping Gilbert's monologue in his haste to get to the point, "what were they *saying*?"

Thomas, you appear to be very red and hot. Red and hot and agitated. Being agitated does not help you to listen. Being calm does help you to listen. Try to be calm.

"As far as I could understand," Gilbert started, in his measured way, "they were saying that the time is very near when the queen, or maybe the tear, from the heavens, must be united with the king from the Earth. That seemed to be important. One of these has been found, the other remains hidden until the time of the stars and the rain. I do not know what that means. Before anything became fully clear, the dream ended, or rather, it changed to a familiar one about losing the ledger and not being able to find it again…"

"Gil, this is really strange," declared Tom, with both excitement and worry in his voice. "Don't you think so? How can we have had the same dream? And how can anyone dream in a language they don't even know? And why do I feel as if we're caught up in something, and we're getting carried along by it?"

He looked at his brother for a reaction, but only the faint frown showed on Gilbert's face.

"To those questions," he replied, gravely, "I have no answer, as yet."

Then, at once, the discussion was interrupted by a jarring metallic clatter, as John began banging lustily on a saucepan with a spoon to signal that the evening meal was ready. To avoid a lecture on punctuality from the Professor, both his sons jumped up to hurry back to the camp. Tom was forced to push away the questions that still crowded in his mind, eager to be asked. As he went, he rubbed at the stings on his hand, which were beginning to tingle all over again as the effects of Willow's salve wore off.

"You have nettle stings on your hand," Gilbert observed, and Tom, slightly shamefaced, told him of his tumble over the tree root. He described Willow's soothing ointment and its wild, herbal scent, but was careful not to mention the exact purpose of his visit to the gypsy camp. Gilbert asked no questions.

As they arrived at the edge of the camp, Gilbert turned to Tom.

"On the subject of *urtica dioica,* the common stinging nettle," he began, "I can tell you of a trivial but peculiar aspect of last night's events. When I went to bed, I was fine, but when I woke up, my right ankle was covered in stings. The explanation which comes to mind, Thomas, is somnambulism, or sleepwalking. And yet, when I got up this morning, my tent door was as tightly laced as ever. Most strange."

Then Gilbert trudged on, and so did not see Tom involuntarily shiver, as if a grey goose had walked over his grave.

Chapter 10

"If they will not give Her, us must take Her. It must be so. There be no other way."

Tinman was rarely afraid. A big, strong man, he was used to protecting his own and fighting off all comers, whoever they be, Gypsy or gaujo, anyone. But this was a matter beyond his strength, beyond the power of muscle and bone and will. Everything he held dear hung in the balance, on the will of strangers – and young ones at that. And so he knew fear, and longed for action. Action he could understand. Waiting he could not.

Willow smiled, for she knew her man well and felt for him in his frustration and fear. But her Knowing told her that to take Her would be wrong, so wrong – it would taint the Joining and then the Power would never arise, the foot would never be set on the path, leaving the way open for the Dark Times to engulf everything. Dark Times, everlasting and unbreakable; the risk they must not take. And yet, she knew how hard the waiting was becoming. She looked to Pigsticker and Mother Bessamy, one inscrutable, one nodding determinedly, and waited for their words. It was Mother Bessamy who spoke.

"We speak of taking Her from them – but there is the Other to consider."

The old woman looked deeply troubled. She had told them of her meeting with the gaujo girl, and shared her surprise and dismay on learning that she, too, seemed to have a part in what was to be. Tinman had turned and spat on the ground, the bitterness of it too much to bear.

Pigsticker stared into the distance, his pipe in his mouth, unlit. Finally, he spoke.

"One more night," he declared, "one night shall pass, and then, we acts."

Willow stared at them all, one by one.

"Then," she declared quietly, "we must hope that we acts rightly – for all our sakes, and the sake of all those to come."

Nightfall came, draping deep, soft darkness over the hills, spreading it over the woods and the village, soothing the sunburnt earth with its cooling touch. It released the night creatures, to pad along their scent-marked trails, to scurry, large-eyed, among the dim, dry grasses or to take to the air on wings, feathered or leathery or powdered, each according to its kind. But the night withheld its usual gift of sleep from many of those who were waiting for it.

In the village, excited children tossed and turned and sighed away the last few hours of waiting for the summer pageant.

In the vicarage, in his plain, clean bedroom, the Reverend Pilcher lay on top of his blanket in his loose cotton nightshirt, thinking of his mission the next day, whispering a brief prayer for its success.

In the Montfalcon mansion, Geraldine lay between crisp starched sheets and hugged a gleeful secret to herself.

On her window ledge, a ragged black and white bird perched unseen. Its wakeful eyes glinted in the starlight, while its beak periodically opened and closed as if silently speaking to an unseen listener.

And in the small camp on the edge of the wood, only the four student workers slept, the weariness of a working day enhanced by the passing round of a half-bottle of brandy, which Wilf had been delighted to find stowed in the bottom of his knapsack – and which his friends had been only too pleased to share with him. Professor Warrington had narrowed his eyes at the sound of their giggling and clumsy shushing. When the noise died away, he continued to frown. He read until midnight, without pleasure, then found himself unable to settle to sleep.

Not again. What the devil's wrong with me? What a miserable waste of time. Too tired to read, too tired to sleep. An insomniac, that's what I'm turning into. A sad, useless insomniac. Damn it all.

A few yards away, behind his own canvas walls, Tom also lay restless, still going over the previous night's strange dream again and again, searching for whatever meaning it might have. But though this was fascinating, it was also exhausting, and soon it gave way to dreamy thoughts of the next day's village pageant and all that Mr Moss had told him about the fun and games.

Please let us go. Please… be in a good mood and let us go. It isn't a lot to ask… one day in a whole summer… please, please, let us go…

In the last inhabited tent, Gilbert lay still in his familiar camp bed, fully awake and busily replaying in every detail the strange speech from the dream, perfectly remembered but becoming no clearer. Accustomed to the darkness, his eyes could make out the bulky shape of his coat, hanging on its makeshift hanger on the tent's corner pole, and concealing the bag in which he kept his precious stone.

It is quiet tonight. Quiet and not calling at all. Not calling for the first time since I found her. Found it. Found her. It is more peaceful without her calling. More peaceful for concentrating. Concentrating on proper things, not on wondering and wishing and everything whirling around. Everything whirling around in a mess and a rush and a headache. Better for thinking when it is quiet. Definitely so.

When morning came, the camp awoke in the light of dawn to scratchy eyes and equally scratchy tempers. The students were sluggish and breakfast was late, the kettle seemed to take forever to boil and even Tom had little to say. For the Professor had said nothing about the pageant at all and, stomping round the camp and muttering under his breath, he seemed to be preparing for a normal day of work.

Tom's disappointment was like a sad and bitter lump lodged in his throat, which he could not shift. Gilbert offered him no comfort. It was his regular day for airing his bedding, and he had set about the dull task as he always did, bringing his blanket outside to shake it, folding it neatly, then returning it to the tent. Next, he took the sheet off the old striped mattress and the cover off the rather hard pillow which he always brought with him from home. Tom felt a rare surge of impatience with Gilbert's routines.

When the scream came from Gilbert's tent, Tom scrambled up, heart racing, and ran to see what on Earth was wrong. He pushed through the tent flap to where his brother stood.

"What is it, Gil? Are you all right?" he asked.

Gilbert looked horrified, holding a limp straggle of greenery in his hands as his sheet crumpled around his feet. Puzzled, Tom stopped in his tracks, while Arthur and John peered round the flap, looking concerned but saying nothing.

"What's that, Gil?' asked Tom, gently, stepping closer to his brother as gently as if he were approaching a cornered animal.

Gilbert's face was white as he looked down at the leaves and stalks in his hands.

"*Urtica dioica,*" he got out, in a strangled whisper, "here, in my sheet."

"Nettles?" Tom asked, confused. "How did they get there?" Gilbert simply shook his head, and stood helplessly, as if in shock.

"Put them down, Gil," said Tom, calmly, "they'll sting your fingers."

Wordlessly, Gilbert let the nettles drop, and Tom, picking them up in a fold of his shirtsleeve, threw them out of the tent.

The colour slowly returned to Gilbert's face and the morning's activity resumed outside in the camp. Without coming in, the Professor called gruffly to enquire whether all was well, and Tom called back that everything was now fine. He then sat beside Gilbert on the stripped bed, to work out how the nettles had come to be lodged in the folds of the sheet.

"At least you know now how your ankle got stung," Tom said, glad in a way to find a simple explanation.

"But how did they get there, and why, Thomas?" asked

Gilbert, and then repeated 'How?' and 'Why?' to himself several times, closing his eyes tightly and pinching the bridge of his nose with his fingers, as he did when most profoundly mystified.

Tom, who had his own suspicions, thought it best to try and distract his brother from the question before it became the only thing he could think about.

"Well, anyway, Gil," he said, "it looks like we're in for a full day's work. Is the ledger set up ready?"

Gilbert took the bait. "The ledger!" he cried, looking up, "I haven't done it!"

"Do it now," suggested Tom, standing up to pass the big leather book to him, knowing that the familiar task would help him to calm down.

Gilbert took the ledger in both hands and closed his eyes, breathing deeply. Reassured, he took it to his small writing desk and laid it carefully down, then sat stiffly on his camp stool, reaching for his pen and ink from their stand.

"Thank you, Thomas," he said, not looking around.

Tom knew that he was no longer needed. He slipped out of the tent, breathing a sigh of relief that the small drama was over. He walked back over to the stove and flopped down in a heap. John shook his head sadly as Tom explained what had happened, then handed him a dented tin plate containing a saved rasher of bacon and the last of the mushrooms.

But breakfast would have to wait, for once again, a sudden cry of distress sounded from Gilbert's tent and again, Tom sprang up and ran to his brother's side.

"Gil!" he called as he pushed through the flap into the tent again. "What on Earth's happened now?"

Gilbert stood beside his desk, both his hands clutched tightly in his hair, his eyes wide and staring with horror.

"Look!" was all he could get out.

"Look at what?" asked Tom, carefully, seeing nothing obviously amiss.

"There," said Gilbert, nodding faintly in the direction of the ledger, his voice quavering.

He began to rock back and forth in his distress, his hands still grasping tightly at the sides of his head. Tom looked down at the ledger, lying open on the little desk, and saw a dark smear disfiguring the clean new page. He bent to look more closely, and his nose wrinkled as he realised that the long, curved mark was in fact the squashed body of a worm that had been trapped between the pages as the book was closed upon it.

"Oh, no, that's horrible," Tom said, looking in disgust at the sticky mess of mud and blood on the fine, creamy paper. "Poor worm. Gil, I think I know who's behind this. Nobody here would do something like that. It has to be Geraldine. She was here yesterday and…"

But Gilbert was not listening. He turned and fled from the sight of the violated ledger and then stood several yards away, outside, rocking and groaning, empty-eyed. Tom stood defensively nearby and when the Professor strode over, explained to him what had happened. Thankfully, rather than shouting at Gilbert, he simply tutted and went to collect the ledger himself, then used his penknife to slice out the offending pages. He stood for a dismal moment watching his son, then turned and headed back to the stone circle, his mood worse than ever.

"Ronald, good morning to you," said Reverend Pilcher,

arriving slightly out of breath from the walk up the slope to the camp.

"Ah, yes, er, um, morning, Toby," the Professor replied, hesitating before turning round, in case his face should show any trace of his emotion. "Didn't expect to see you today," he went on, before the Reverend could speak, "thought you'd be taken up with this pageant business, whatever that may be about…"

"Well, yes, in a way I am," his friend replied, "because that's what I want to talk to you about."

Looking the Professor in the eye, the vicar gently but firmly began to persuade him that he, his workers and most of all, his sons, really needed a day of rest and fun and enjoyment, and that attending the pageant would do them all a power of good.

Twenty minutes later, the two men walked back from the stones to the camp and Professor Warrington called everyone together. He announced that work was to be curtailed at midday to allow the afternoon and evening to be spent in the village. The students were delighted and Tom was overjoyed. He raced round the company in circles, whooping and jumping up to punch the air, making everybody laugh, even Gilbert and the Professor. Reverend Pilcher silently thanked his God.

Spurred on by the promise of an afternoon and evening of fun and games, the archaeological team worked with a will through the warm morning. At noon, they happily downed tools, spruced themselves up and set off together down to the village to see what was afoot. On the way, they practised a few riddles, just in case they should be asked any when they arrived, for Tom had warned them about the dunking in the horse trough that would follow a wrong answer.

Gilbert alone did not share in the fun of the riddling. He listened intently to the puzzling words, and the accompanying groans and laughter, and the frown line deepened between his eyes. Tom saw his hands beginning to twitch and flap, down by his sides, never a good sign. Gilbert turned to Tom with deep confusion showing on his face.

"Why are they doing that?" he asked. "Why are they asking each other questions, when they know the answer already, and the people whom they are asking do not?'

Tom opened his mouth to answer, but Gilbert went on.

"That is backwards," he said. "When you ask a question, you *should not* know the answer, and the person whom you are asking *should*. Otherwise it is not logical. It makes no sense."

Tom realised the truth of his brother's words and tried to think how to explain the purpose of a riddle.

"Well…" he said slowly, feeling for the words, "it's not really about getting your question answered… it's more about showing that you're cleverer than the person you're asking, because you get it and they don't."

"Oh," said Gilbert and continued to walk along, thinking this over.

Eventually, Gilbert looked up at Tom with a slightly happier look on his face.

"I do know one riddle," he informed him, "I have just remembered it, though I first read it in a collection of classical legends when I was eleven years and three months old."

Tom looked over at him expectantly, waiting to hear what it might be. But Gilbert simply nodded slightly and carried on walking, keeping his riddle to himself alone.

I wonder whether anyone knows Willow's riddle? I'm not going to ask, though... I think it's something I'm supposed to do by myself.

As the party reached the road, they joined with a small stream of people heading for the pageant from farms and villages all around. The throng walked along together in high spirits, adults laughing and joking together, children and dogs running in and out and getting under everybody's feet. When a motor-car horn sounded behind them, the walkers parted to let the vehicle through and openly admired its gleaming paint and brass. In the back of the car sat Geraldine and her father, waving like royalty. Tom felt sick.

Oh, no, not her. Just let her stay away from me, for I've a few things to say to her... You may think you've got away with everything again, Geraldine, but I know it was you and I'll give you what you deserve...

But even as he plotted his revenge, Tom was painfully aware that, as ever, the upper hand was with the red-haired girl in the smart black car, and he burned with the frustration of defeat.

Luckily, the sight of the village decked out for the pageant was enough to make Tom's eyes widen and the memory of Geraldine fade. The green was garlanded with bunting, dotted with stalls and tents and crowded with people – more people than he had seen together in one place in a long time. Just as Mr Moss had said, some of them wore costumes. Shrieks arose as a hobby horse frisked around, butting and biting, while a jester, a moth-eaten dragon and two or three knights in knitted armour chased each other round and round. Several lords and ladies paraded proudly, even though their finery had clearly seen better days.

Tom smiled as he caught the strains of music amongst the hubbub of voices and the cries of the stallholders: morris tunes, played on accordion and drum. The morris men clacked hefty sticks together as they hopped and skipped along the road and into their place on the green. Meanwhile, Gilbert took a few minutes to prepare himself to go among so many people and such a lot of noise.

Tom stood beside him, waiting, savouring the rare feeling of having money to spend. To his delight, his father had handed him a few coins and told him to enjoy himself however he saw fit. Gilbert checked that he and Tom had exactly the same amount and was pleased that they did. Gilbert had decided that the best idea would be to walk round and see all the stalls and games and booths before deciding how to spend their limited funds. Tom had to agree with his brother's wisdom, though, given the choice, he would have plunged into a glorious, reckless spree – and probably been penniless within five minutes.

Gilbert committed the list of stalls to memory as he walked around, classifying them neatly in his orderly mind.

Category one: food and drink. Lemonade with paper twists of sugar, cider from stone jars. Home-baked biscuits, cakes and fruit pies; toffee, gingerbread men and peppermint pigs. Category two: games and challenges: swing boats, tombola, test-your-strength. Bat the rat, crockery shy, skittle alley. Throw a wet sponge at the postmaster, as he puts his face through a hole in a painted scene which makes him resemble a mermaid... why? Reverend Pilcher's bran tub. A prize every time. Not very challenging. Why not just buy the prize and avoid the dusty bran?

"I just can't decide what to do!" Tom exclaimed.

He jumped aside as a greased piglet galloped madly by, chased by a straggle of panting boys. Jack Hibbert's huge shire horse, Old Ben, could be seen plodding up and down the field with two little girls sitting on his broad back. His polished harness and gleaming brasses made him look like some kind of heroic warhorse, loaded with medals.

"Then I suggest, Thomas, that you think for a short while longer," Gilbert suggested helpfully. Then he added, "I myself have found the challenge which most appeals to me."

Saying this, he made for a small, unobtrusive stall with a plain handwritten sign that read 'Guess the weight of the cake'. On display was a fine, large Dundee cake decorated with almonds and smelling faintly of allspice. Gilbert paid for his turn and considered the cake most carefully.

"I may be some time," he warned Tom, "you might prefer to carry on without me and I will wait here for you to return."

Then, he sat on the grass and took out his notebook and pencil from his waistcoat pocket, and, under the bemused eye of the lady stallholder, he began muttering and writing questions and figures on the page. Tom heard him saying to himself, "Now, butter, flour, sugar, fruit, eggs... what would be the average weight of an egg?"

Gilbert sat contentedly, sucking the pencil hard as he worked over the question in his mind. Smiling, Tom left him to it, and headed off to spend the money that was burning a hole in his pocket.

CHAPTER 11

As Tom enjoyed a most satisfying afternoon batting rats, smashing crockery, gorging on sweets and chasing around with a bunch of village boys dressed as sailors, Geraldine was also in her element. She had easily managed to slip away from her father, whose company she found utterly boring, and had taken out her camera and begun photographing the festivities. She was quite prepared to order her subjects to pose or move as she wanted, and she soon captured the hobby horse, a juggler and several lordly couples. She caught the vicar unawares, mid-sneeze. But all of this was a diversion, concealing her true purpose.

Come on, Gypsies, show yourselves! I know you hate to be photographed, heaven knows why, but I must insist, so come on... drag yourselves away from your fakery and pocket-picking and stand for the camera...

But the Gypsies were nowhere to be found; not at the far end of the village where a few horses were being traded, or among the stalls where they would normally be selling potions and clothes pegs, or anywhere else. At last, a frustrated Geraldine was forced to give up the search and stop for a drink, for the afternoon had become very hot. She purchased a raspberry cordial and took it to a bench where she could sit and sip it without being jostled by the elbows of the careless crowd.

But as she watched the costumed fools with some distaste, Geraldine was dismayed to see that one of them was coming to share her bench with her. A morris dancer, maybe – he wore a tattered coat of coloured rags and his face was darkened with black greasepaint and shaded by a battered, lumpy old hat. Raising his glass cheerily, he sat down next to her just as if he had been invited.

"Your ladyship," he said, in an old man's voice, with a little salute which might or might not have been mockery, it was difficult to tell.

Has your coat never seen the inside of a laundry, old man? You smell like a rancid badger.

"'Tis a fine day," the old man announced, trying again to gain her attention. He looked sideways at her with a grin. "A fine day for a pageant," he tried again, while Geraldine merely looked at him with disdain.

What a marvellous talent for dullness! As a village idiot, you could win a prize.

"A fine day for a few riddles," the man persisted, at which point Geraldine felt she had to stop him.

"Excuse me," she said, in a tone which made it clear she would stand no nonsense, "but I have come here to enjoy a moment's peace. I would be grateful if you would permit me to continue uninterrupted."

At this, the old man's face twitched briefly, but he swiftly put his smile back into place and carried on regardless.

"'Tis riddling day!" he insisted. "None can say no to a riddle today. Answer me this, your ladyship, then I shall leave you to your peace."

Without waiting for her approval, the old man launched into a rhyme in his creaky, country voice:

"He hops like a frog, but no frog he;
He'll steal your gold and finery.
Off he'll fly with your finest jewel;
His heart is black and his eye is cruel.
He's a clever one, but you can't teach him,
Try to catch him – you'll not reach him.
He'll caw and cackle, he'll boast and brag –
So tell me, who's the chatternag?"

Geraldine sighed impatiently as the old man finished his riddle and waited for her to answer.

"Oh, please, do let me think," she said, making a show of closing her eyes and holding her fingers to her temple as if deep in thought. After a short pause, she announced, "No, I am afraid I simply cannot work that out. Pray tell me the answer to your fascinating riddle."

But as she opened her eyes and turned to give the old man a mocking smile, Geraldine was so startled that she gasped and jumped, and the pink cordial spattered her pristine white clothes. For the old man was gone as if into thin air. In his place sat a tattered heap of black and white feathers that was horribly familiar. She recoiled as the creature raised a bony claw to scratch at the side of its head, then opened its beak to reveal its horrid black tongue.

"Kaaark!" it announced.

Geraldine exclaimed in disgust, leapt to her feet, snatched up her camera and ran from the place, silently cursing the old man and the revolting bird, and disgusted by her damp, stained skirts, which clung stickily to her skin as she ran.

But there was to be no escape for Miss Montfalcon. Wherever she went, whatever space she ducked into or however she tried to conceal herself in the crowd, the unkempt old bird was never far away. It bounced along beside her when she tried to walk away from it, sat in front of her so she had to step over it, and flapped past her ear when she thought she had left it behind. Once, it appeared right in her face, riding on the shoulder of a costumed boy who came towards her out of the crowd. The magpie let loose a stream of mocking cackles and Geraldine gasped. As the bird flapped and bounded away, the boy laughed, only stopping when he realised that Geraldine, thoroughly annoyed, was on the point of slapping him.

If I catch that repulsive bird, I'll wring its neck! Or would, if I had my gloves on.

In the meantime, Tom had popped back several times to the guess-the-weight-of-the-cake stall, to check on Gilbert's progress. Each time, Gilbert was deep in thought, drawing small charts and diagrams or scribbling figures in his book.

"Allow for evaporation..." he murmured to himself, adjusting a couple of numbers with his pencil.

The lady who was running the stall looked at Tom with a puzzled expression on her face. Tom just smiled at her and shrugged, knowing it would be impossible to explain Gilbert's ways. He remarked that the cake looked delicious and then, promising to return in about half an hour, went back to the pleasures of the festival.

By now, some of the stalls were just about empty, their goods sold out, and the games and sideshows were beginning to wind down towards a close. However, the test-your-strength machine was still drawing a crowd. Tom saw that Mr Moss the blacksmith was about to take his turn and he hurried closer, weaving through the groups of onlookers to watch what was clearly becoming a drama.

Go on Mr Moss! Go on!

The blacksmith was playing to the audience like a circus strongman. Rather than simply stepping up to the plate with the mallet, striking the plate and seeing how far up the pole the metal ball would go, he was whirling the huge hammer round his head like a battle-mad Viking with his axe. The crowd looked on, eyes shining, as the mallet spun faster and faster, slicing the air, and the feeling of danger grew. Then, all at once, the onlookers caught their breath as the mallet flew up into the sky, spinning end-over-end in the early-evening sun. When the handle landed squarely in the smith's strong, hard hands they all breathed out together in relief and broke into a storm of clapping and whistling.

Brilliant!

The smith grinned at the crowd as they edged back into place, then took his turn at the machine. Swish, bang, and the ball raced upwards, the bell rang out, and Mr Moss roared again in triumph. The crowd all cheered to see their champion claim his prize, just as he did every year.

Meanwhile, far from the noise and excitement of the competition, Gilbert had reached the end of his workings out and was ready to present his conclusion. Standing up a little stiffly, he turned to address the lady stallholder. She was being very patient, but for the last twenty minutes had been wanting to award the prize, pack up the little stall and go home to get ready for the evening's entertainment. She watched Gilbert check his notebook one last time.

"My estimate of the weight of this cake," he announced, "based on my calculations, is four pounds, three and three-quarter ounces."

Then he stood back and smiled just slightly, waiting.

"Well, fancy that!" the lady exclaimed. "I don't know how you did it, young man, but you're barely a pennyweight out. Nobody's guessed closer than that! And you didn't even pick the cake up to test it!"

"Is that allowed?" asked Gilbert.

"It's what most folks do, yes," she said, considering this obvious.

She swiftly placed the cake in a box, handed it over to its winner, and rapidly dismantled the stall, ready to leave. Left standing alone, holding his prize, Gilbert was very content indeed.

A most successful afternoon. A satisfying challenge, a fine cake to take back to camp, and money remaining for another day. Yes, a most successful afternoon.

He sat on the grass where the stall had been and opened the lid of the cake box so he could look at his prize while waiting for Tom to arrive. Even when Geraldine appeared, it was not enough to spoil his mood. She came stamping along, carrying her camera case, pinkish stains blotting her once-white dress. Even more strangely, she was accompanied by a magpie, which seemed to be missing its tail.

"*Pica pica!*" said Gilbert out loud, before he could stop himself, and Geraldine halted, right in front of him. She looked down to where he sat with the open box on his lap.

"Nuts," she announced, looking at the fine rounds of roasted almonds that decorated the top of the cake. "How appropriate."

"Hello, Miss Geraldine Montfalcon," Gilbert got out, unsure of what else he could say. Geraldine looked down her nose at him.

"Not playing with the Gypsies today?" she asked, with a meaningful edge in her voice.

"No," he said, "the Gypsies are not here. They have their own festival, in the wood."

"Oh, do they really? Fancy that!" said Geraldine, all polite interest for once. "At their campsite, I suppose?" she asked, innocently.

"I don't know exactly where," said Gilbert, "but yes, somewhere near the camp, I expect."

"I wonder what they do there?" she asked, musingly. "It must be very interesting to be worth missing the pageant for."

"I don't know about it," Gilbert replied, truthfully. Then he looked again at the magpie, which was now preening and nibbling at its scruffy feathers and twitching its head from side to side.

"Why have you got a magpie with you?" he asked. "Did you win it?"

"No, I most certainly did not!" she snapped back. "It's nothing but a pest, the hideous thing. I'm trying to get rid of it, but it's too stupid to know where it's not wanted."

She rolled her eyes and flounced away.

That girl is ignorant. The bird is not stupid. Magpies are members of the corvid family and all corvids are very intelligent. Relative to body-weight, it probably has more brain than she does.

Gilbert watched Geraldine go, the magpie hopping and fluttering alongside, then firmly put her out of his mind.

Shortly after this, a very excited Tom arrived at the tea tent in a rowdy procession with Gilbert, who carried his cake in its box, and the students, all laughing uproariously in a cider-scented way. Reverend Pilcher and the Professor were waiting for them, having whiled away a couple of pleasant hours with ale and talk. The vicar gathered more stools so that they could all sit down. Then he listened as they told their tales of the afternoon's exploits and Tom gabbled out the story of the smith's spectacular show. He admired Tom's prizes from the day, including a small box with a hole in the bottom, which could be made to look as if it contained a severed finger. The Professor pulled a face, then, for once, laughed.

Then Gilbert showed his prize.

"The stall was called 'Guess the Weight of the Cake,'" he explained, "and the stallholder said that most people just pick up the cake and then try to guess what it might weigh. But there is no need to guess when you can work it out properly instead."

He took out his notebook and showed and explained the figures and scribbles – 'average weight of a raisin', 'number of nuts per cubic inch' and many more – which had finally brought him to the correct answer.

"That's my boy," said the Professor, smiling approval at his elder son.

Gilbert looked back at him blankly and the Professor's

smile died away. Then the company noisily broke up amid cheers and hoots of laughter. John had just given a ridiculously wrong answer to a riddle and was carried out to the horse trough, struggling and laughing, and dropped in.

"Most refreshing!" declared Reverend Pilcher, and the word turned his mind to thoughts of another beer, which the Professor obligingly brought.

Although it had become the habit in the village to refer to the summer festival as 'The Pageant', in truth the pageant itself was only one part of the proceedings. A play that was more like a pantomime, it was the highlight of the evening and it never failed to draw a good crowd.

This year, the theme was to be the Battle of the Nile, Nelson's victory over Napoleon's French navy, in memory of the village celebrations over a century before. Tom had learned from the sailor boys that the final scene of the play would be very dramatic indeed, so he found a good spot at the edge of the crowd and left Gilbert's cake with Reverend Pilcher so that they would not have to be careful of it during the play. Then they settled to waiting, munching on gingerbread men bought with some of Gilbert's pennies, Tom's being long gone.

And so the pageant was played out before the eager crowd. It roughly told the story of Nelson's naval triumph, but added plenty of mocked-up Frenchmen wearing fake moustaches and strings of onions, hairy-legged men stuffed into ill-fitting dresses, popular songs and romantic scenes which set the ladies sighing and the men booing and cat-calling. Old jokes and in-jokes, chorus lines and muddled lines all flowed merrily, scene after scene, and the audience joined in freely, often raising more laughs than the actors themselves.

But in the eyes of Tom Warrington, and every other boy in the crowd, the pageant's finest moment was the climactic battle between the French and English navies. The sailor boys had secretly armed themselves with real weaponry: bursting flour bags and stolen onions for cannonballs and unripe crab apples for musket balls. Sailing 'ships' made from light wooden cut-outs slung from pairs of shoulder straps like braces, the two sides launched into a wild and frenzied conflict. Caught up in the drama, Tom called out and cheered as flour flew and onions thudded into flesh, leaving bruises and even the odd drop of real blood.

Finally, the French 'ships' were sunk, their sailors lying in a woeful, groaning heap on the deck, while Napoleon slunk away, beaten and shamed. The triumphant English sailor boys called out, "St. George and Merry England!" while their mothers looked horrified and their fathers grinned.

After a final rousing and patriotic speech from Lord Nelson, the crowd cheered and clapped heartily, the actors bowed all together, and the pageant was truly over. After a few moments, the people who had been watching started to get up and drift away, heading for home or the pub, or strolling over to where a huge bonfire had been lit and was beginning to glow.

"Well!" exclaimed Tom, turning to Gilbert, his face shining with joy. "Wasn't that great! The battle, I mean. I wish I'd been in it!"

He acted out hurling a bursting flour bomb, complete

with the sound of it landing smack on the bows of a French warship. Several passers-by smiled at his excitement, but Gilbert was unmoved.

"I am not sure," he said thoughtfully, "that Napoleon was actually present at the Battle of the Nile. I must look it up when I next visit Father's library, to be certain. Do you know, Thomas, I will be pleased to see the library again. I will admit that I miss it when we are in the field."

Only Gilbert. Only Gilbert could watch the best onion fight that ever was – and then say how much he missed a library! I'd exchange five minutes of fun like that for a lifetime in a library. Give me an onion on the head any day, rather than all those dusty old books and endless, unbroken silence...

"Gil!" Tom gasped. "That's it! The riddle!"

Uncertain of what his brother was referring to, Gilbert looked at him rather blankly and waited for him to continue.

"Willow's riddle, I mean – she asked me one the other day," Tom explained. "It was, 'What breaks when you say it?' It must be silence. Silence breaks when you say it! Silence breaks when you say anything! That's good, isn't it?"

"Yes, that is rather ingenious," Gilbert replied after a pause. "It uses an ambiguous sentence to hide a double meaning, and is quite baffling until you understand it, at which point, it becomes obvious."

"Er, yes," Tom said, though he was really only half listening, as he had suddenly remembered how much he had wanted to speak to Pigsticker. It had gone out of his head in all the excitement of the day. But before he could say a word, a strong arm in a familiar, tattered sleeve was there around his shoulders, and a warm, brown, burring voice spoke in his ear.

"Master Thomas!" it said. "Might you be having a moment to spare?"

"Pigsticker!" exclaimed Tom, delighted, turning around to see the old Gypsy there, looking just as he always did, in his mottled, earth-coloured trousers and coat. "How did you know I..."

"Evening, Mister Gilbert," said the old man, cutting him off, touching the brim of his battered old hat in a gesture of respect. "Now, hear this; I needs the help of two young men, on this fine evening, for a most important job that cannot wait."

Tom smiled at this, remembering that he had heard very similar words before, not so long ago.

"What does the job involve?" asked Gilbert. "Should I bring my cake?"

"Oh, it's just a walk to go fetch something," Pigsticker replied, "and maybe a bit of business after. Don't need nothing with you but your wits, and best you never go nowhere without them, anyways."

And with that, Pigsticker set off, moving quickly and smoothly through the last of the crowd, and after a moment, the boys strode off after him, not wishing to be left behind.

Walking away from the village, it soon became clear that Pigsticker's path led back towards the Professor's camp, up the hill towards the woods. Tom walked quickly to catch up with the old man, but when he started to ask a question, Pigsticker looked at him from under the shadowy brim of his hat and put a finger briefly to his lips, signalling for silence. Tom could barely contain his curiosity, but knew that he must wait before any answers would come his way.

What's happening now? Is this going to be an adventure, or just an errand? I hope it's something exciting…

Gilbert simply trudged along, asking nothing, and so it was an unusually quiet trio that climbed the stile as the light began to fade, and then stopped to look back towards the village. The bonfire on the green was just starting to send sparks and smoke up into the sky, and a reddish glow was becoming visible at its heart. Away from the crowds, Pigsticker was prepared to say a little more about the task in hand.

"'Tis like this, see," he began, "there's this… thing, and it's a thing of some considerable value, that is needed from time to time by certain persons, for a particular purpose. Only, this thing has something of a mind of its own, and 'tis a mite choosy as to who it lets find it. And them as finds it don't own it, not never, for it goes where it will. But where it most wants to go, it needs hands to take it, and the hands has to be the proper ones, and the time has to be right, besides. You follow?"

"No," said Tom, mystified, "I don't understand at all! What is the thing and what does all the rest mean, please?"

Gilbert just stood waiting, his brow creasing slightly and his hands just beginning to twitch uneasily.

"Ah," said Pigsticker, "then, let's put it this way round. Maybe you might have had a rare stroke of luck with all that digging you's been doing, and maybe you might have found a certain something a bit special down one o' them holes? A particular thing that looks like a stone but weighs like old iron? 'Bout so big," (here he gestured with his hands together and cupped) "and with something of a way of taking hold of a person, unawares, like? Maybe, you might have found a little something like that?"

Tom's heart leapt.

He knows!

"The stone," said Gilbert, gravely. "We have indeed found it. Only, I believe it is more rightly called 'she' than 'it.'"

Pigsticker's face broke into a grin, but his eyes remained serious.

"Then well found to you, sir," the old man replied, "for She don't be letting herself fall into any old hands. 'Tis an honour to be a Finder, for that's what we calls them She favours, and you has found Her at just the right time. But..." here his voice lowered, becoming more ominous, "the Finder must also be the Giver, and can you do it, I asks you? 'Tis no easy thing to be Giver, that I know. But the time is almost upon us, and She must go to where She needs to be, and She must be taken by the proper hands with right words spoken. You who has found Her, can you let Her go? Will you give Her into those hands?"

He stood looking at Gilbert and Tom, calm and steadfast as ever, but with a clear challenge in his words.

"'Tis for good," he added, quietly, and then he said no more, leaving the double-edged words hanging in the air.

CHAPTER 12

That's hard for Gil. He loves that stone, or anyway, feels something for it. He looks upset, but he's not saying anything. I'll have to leave him be for a while and see if he'll talk to me then. He might not be able to give it up. And what then? What is it about that stone anyway?

Wanting answers, Tom caught up with Pigsticker.

"It was the stone I wanted to ask you about," he said, "I knew there was something unusual about it. But I didn't know it was so special. How can it choose when to be found, and why is it so important that it gets found now and not some other time?"

"I'll tell you this much," Pigsticker replied, when Tom finally drew breath, "that stone is a kind of wonder, something like a legend for us. She don't show up twice in a lifetime, and maybe not even once. But every summer, we remembers Her, and looks for Her to come again. We tells the story of the king and the queen, and we takes care to say the words and pass on the story to the young ones, so that they can know of Her too. And that's what our festival's about, see – but it has to be done in the sky's own time."

"That's like what Willow said," Tom replied.

He looked in puzzlement at the sky, where tiny pinpoint stars were now showing through as the dusky light faded.

"But how does the sky tell you when it's time for the festival?" he asked. "How do you know that this is the right time?"

"Ah, now," said Pigsticker, stopping in his tracks, so suddenly that the boys almost collided with him. "That's what your Pa's not been able to make out yet, for all his book-learning and all his long talking with his friend the good priest. Them stones tells us when. That's how we knows. But you has to know what to look for."

Gilbert started, shaken out of his dazed state.

"The stones!" he exclaimed, with the beginnings of excitement. "If I am correct, you are stating that they are a timekeeping device, or calendar, of which you know the workings. Is it so?"

"I'd not quite say so much, Mister Gilbert," said Pigsticker, guardedly, "but put them stones together with the stars, and there it is. They finds the right night between them, and we goes by what they says."

"But, but…" Tom burst out, "how does it work?"

Pigsticker looked at him long and steadily, and at Gilbert, who was lost for words and simply stood wide-eyed, overwhelmed by what he had heard.

"Not many knows," he said, in a low voice, "but Finders may see the way of it… though we has never before known two Finders together," he added, as an afterthought, "usually 'tis only one; but then, She has her own ways…"

Then he came back to the matter in hand.

"Look up," he said.

Both brothers did so. After a moment he asked them, "What do you see?"

At once, Gilbert began, in his familiar way, to name

the stars and the constellations that were just beginning to glint in the summer night sky. Tom soon sighed and gave up looking.

"It's no good," he said to Pigsticker, as Gilbert continued to recite the litany of names, "I've never learnt all that. Gilbert knows much more about the stars than I do. I only know a few of the constellations, just the easy ones, and I don't really know what I'm looking for."

Gilbert knows more about most things than I do. I'll never be as clever as he is.

Pigsticker looked at Tom for a few moments before answering this, his expression steady, appraising.

"Don't be so sure about that," he said, "just try looking with different eyes."

Tom looked at him quizzically.

"Don't look for naming," the old Gypsy recommended, "look for Knowing. See what you need to see; what's there for you, not what somebody else says is there. Look well now, for the time will never be better."

So, not understanding but willing to try, Tom once again stared up into the cloudless blue heavens with their speckling of stars. He stared for a long time, hoping to see, and gradually, gently, the distant stars began to draw him in. He got a sense that somehow, they knew he was there, and were shining especially for him. Gilbert's voice faded into the distance, leaving Tom with the feeling that he was quite alone with the stars. They felt more real and close than they had ever been before. He could almost have reached out and touched them with his fingers.

And then it happened. Without any star moving from its place at all, the patterns in the darkening sky subtly shifted and altered, and instead of the familiar groupings and figures, Tom saw each star as separate, alone and entirely itself. And then, before his wondering eyes, a different pattern formed. Some stars glowed brighter than ever, others modestly dimmed, until a new constellation emerged, spreading triumphantly across the vast night sky.

Clear as clear, the exact pattern of the ring stones shone out, that familiar jagged circle and tail that had consumed their thoughts by day and haunted their dreams at night. And Tom was thrilled by the unearthly beauty of it.

"So, Master Thomas," declared Pigsticker, when finally, a stiff neck made Tom reluctantly return to Earth and the three of them continued along the path and back towards the Professor's camp, "now you has seen what few folks knows how to see. They has the eyes, you see, but not the heart."

Tom was warmed by the old man's words, though he hoped that Gilbert wouldn't take them too hard. Gilbert had not seen the pattern of the stones emerge among the stars, and was puzzled by Tom's description of it.

"But how could Ursa Major have disappeared?" he had asked, when Tom had tried to explain that the normal constellations had seemed to dissolve away.

"It didn't disappear," Tom said, feeling that he had not told it rightly at all, "I just couldn't see it any more. It was still there, just... not there," he finished, rather lamely.

Gilbert looked at him in confusion.

That is most contrary. I would not wish to see the constellations gone. Something that is gone cannot be seen. I like the stars the way they are, and would rather that they stayed in their proper forms, and in the places where they belong.

Tom was relieved when Gilbert turned to trudge onward, asking no more questions.

When they arrived at the camp it was deserted, as the archaeological team had stayed in the village for the evening's festivities. Gilbert halted outside his tent. He had not been able to bring himself to agree to parting with his stone, though neither had he said that he wouldn't. The decision was terrible for him, and he had gone stubbornly silent when Tom had tried to help him to make up his mind. Tom had not liked the distant look in his brother's eyes, nor the grim set of his mouth, nor the twitching of his hands.

Come on, Gil. You can do this. Pigsticker wouldn't ask if it weren't important. You know that stone has something strange about it – let him have it before it turns your mind...

Pigsticker and Tom lingered in the shadows, at a respectful distance, to allow Gilbert to do as he had to do. While they waited, Tom questioned Pigsticker about the mysterious stone.

"Where did it come from?" he asked.

"Ah, well," Pigsticker said, "they say She came straight out of the sky, long, long ago, blazing red and trailing a banner like fire behind Her. 'Tis said that She came down so hard, She was drove into the ground, in a smoking hole, and when the first Finder came to prise Her out, She was still burning hot."

Pleased to be having his question answered, Tom pressed the old Gypsy further.

"So, is it – she – always found round here, and always buried in the ground?"

"Since that first Finding, She has come and gone as She pleases," Pigsticker replied, "sometimes She is underground, or in a stream, or just in the grass. But if you ain't the Finder, you could be standing on top of Her and not know She was there. She only goes to those she chooses, see."

Then, Pigsticker fell silent and smiled. Gilbert had gone into his tent and lit the candle. As they waited for him to bring out the stone, Tom heard whispered words which were joltingly familiar.

"That which was lost, now is found."

There was a very long pause before Gilbert emerged from the tent. When he came, he had both hands clasped to his chest, holding tightly to his burden. He walked towards his brother and Pigsticker in silence, each step painfully slow and heavy. When he grew close enough to see clearly, Tom was horrified by the desolate look that was etched onto his brother's face. His eyes stared blankly and his mouth was drawn down hard by utter misery.

"Gil!" said Tom, urgently, taking one careful step towards him. "Whatever's wrong?"

But Gilbert didn't answer. All at once, he put his head down and roared an almighty roar, then charged as fast as he could towards the trees. Tom was taken by surprise, for he rarely if ever saw Gilbert run. Before either he or Pigsticker could act, Gilbert had thrashed his way clumsily into the wood and disappeared from view.

"I must go after him!" Tom gasped out, tugging Pigsticker's sleeve to make him follow. But Pigsticker threw an arm round him and held him back.

"No!" he said firmly.

What?

Tom felt his stomach lurch at the sudden change in Pigsticker's manner. He had never known the old man to be so commanding and his voice suggested that he expected to be obeyed. Tom looked uneasily at his stony face, not quite daring to defy him but desperate to go after his brother. After a few moments, Pigsticker lowered his arm.

"We shall find him better with ears than with eyes in this elf-light," he explained in something more like his usual voice, and Tom did not protest.

Pigsticker cocked his head to listen closely, and, though Tom could hear nothing but the pounding of his own heart, the Gypsy seemed satisfied.

"Come quietly," Pigsticker ordered.

He set off, moving carefully in the direction he knew Gilbert to have taken. He passed among the long grass and bracken without so much as a swish, and Tom tried to follow just as soundlessly himself. Before long, he realised that they were catching up with Gilbert, who was moving more slowly now, scuffing through the undergrowth on heavy feet, breathing in ragged sobs. But before Tom could begin to make out his brother's form among the dark shadows of the trees, he was stopped in his tracks. A sudden scream sounded out just ahead, and was almost immediately cut off, leaving the woods in silence, shocked.

Gil!

Terrified, Tom looked to Pigsticker, who signalled him to wait and to be quiet. Tom tried to follow his command, and stood as still as he could, crossing his fingers and toes until they hurt.

"Leave him be," Pigsticker called out into the darkness, the authority of a few minutes before back in his voice again.

He stepped forward, speaking clearly in the Romany language. Almost at once, three figures emerged from the shadows. One, small and stooped, spoke back in the same tongue, while the other, tall and broad, stood quiet, holding Gilbert firmly by the collar. In the darkness Tom could see that his brother's face was white and his breath came in whimpers. Pigsticker spoke again, and the figure released Gilbert, who stood staring blankly, his hands still clutching tightly to the object he held against his heart.

"Tinman!" exclaimed Tom, coming close enough to see more clearly.

Tinman looked at him once, then turned away and coughed a little, as if embarrassed. The old woman who stood beside him spoke for them both.

"So the Finder will not be the Giver," she declared, "and he tried to run with Her and take Her away from Her rightful place. We cannot let this be, Pigsticker, as we has said before. We cannot let the *gaujo* destroy this night. If he will not give Her, we must take Her ourselves! What other way can there be?"

The old woman flung out an angry, accusing arm towards Gilbert. The silver of a blade flashed in her outstretched hand. Tom gasped. Gilbert continued to stare blankly past her as if she did not exist. The knife glinted subtly in the gloom and Tom's breath caught in his throat. He swallowed hard and gathered his courage to speak.

"Let… let me talk to him," he managed to get out, "he can't talk to anyone else when he goes like that. Let me try. Please!"

The three Gypsies exchanged looks. Then Pigsticker nodded.

"Ask him," he said, "if he will *please* return the stone, for all our sakes, not least his own."

"I will try," Tom replied, and then walked over to where Gilbert was standing, empty-eyed and slightly trembling.

Tom knew better than to touch him or face him head on. Instead, he stood to one side and simply repeated "Gilbert" over and over again, in a soft voice, until finally the life came back into his brother's face and he was able to listen and speak once more.

"They need the stone, Gil," Tom said gently.

Gilbert was clutching the stone's carrying bag so tightly that his hands were hidden in the twists of fabric. Looking down at it, his legs at once gave way under him and he collapsed to the ground, to bury his head in his arms and weep.

"I know!" he wailed, his voice rough and raw with anguish. "I went to bring her, but… she's gone!"

He threw the cloth bag at Tom's feet, where it lay, flat and empty. A stunned silence fell. Tom's mind worked furiously.

Oh no! Where's it gone? Oh… I think I know.

"Geraldine!" he exclaimed. "It has to be. She must have taken it."

"The squire's daughter," said Pigsticker, considering

this most seriously. "You was right then, Mother Bessamy. She do have a part to play. But why would she have taken the stone to herself, I wonders?"

"Just to be nasty," said Tom, decisively. "She's horrible to us, especially Gilbert. She picks on him, does things like putting nettles in his bed and muddling him up with questions, and he can't fight back. And we have to be nice to her, because otherwise her father will throw us off the site, and then our father would never forgive us. And she loves it, because she is Princess Geraldine and she never gets in any trouble at all…"

"She's in trouble now," Pigsticker said, in a dark tone, "trouble like she's never known in her life. Listen, Master Thomas, and listen well. The matter of this stone goes beyond a rich young lady's foolish games. If that stone ain't where She needs to be this very night, all that lives will suffer for it. Dark Times is coming to this land, Master Thomas, and we must do all that is needful; for them that stands against that darkness will need all their strength about them, and the stone is a part of it. It must be found and brought back, for the time is coming in, and many is waiting."

"We have to find Geraldine then," said Tom, understanding the urgency of Pigsticker's words, though some of their meaning remained obscure.

"And you must comfort and strengthen your brother, for he is another part of this, and much depends upon him," Pigsticker replied.

Indeed, Gilbert still looked stricken.

"She was gone from me, and I did not look to her," he was saying, as if to himself, "gone from me, and I did not question it. I did not question why she was quiet. Why, why, why?"

Sunk in misery, Gilbert rocked to and fro, his head in his hands. Tom sat by him, knowing better than to try to ask questions or intervene. Waiting was the only thing that would help him, but to Tom, time suddenly felt horribly short.

Pigsticker talked in quiet, urgent Romany with Mother Bessamy and the Tinman and then watched the two of them leave in the darkness. Tom occupied himself with his own thoughts, wondering about the mysterious stone.

What does he mean, she was quiet? Stones are always quiet, are they not? How can a stone be anything but quiet? This is all extremely strange.

By the time Gilbert was calm, Pigsticker had made a small fire and was sitting beside it, more for its light than its heat. His pipe was lit, and blue-grey smoke hung in scented wisps in the warm night air. The brothers sat facing him and Tom asked how they were to find Geraldine.

"Ah," said Pigsticker, tapping his nose with his finger as he had done before, "there is ways and means. We has a pair of beady eyes on that girl, eyes that don't miss much and ain't easy to get out from under. Kapchak's watching her for us, at Mother Bessamy's bidding, and he shall tell us what we needs to know."

"Who's Kapchak?" asked Tom, never having heard the name among his Gypsy friends, or anywhere else.

"You'll see," Pigsticker replied.

He stood up, cupped his hands around his mouth and whistled shrilly into the evening air.

"He'll not be long," he said, "and then we shall see what

we shall see. That's what Mother Bessamy says," he added, "she's the fortune teller, you know."

"Oh!" said Tom. "I remember, Geraldine went to see her. She said she was…" and he stopped himself there, and felt heat rise in his face.

"Said she was what?" asked Pigsticker, sharply.

"She said she was… a charlatan," admitted Tom, sorry to have to say it.

"Oh, did she now?" Pigsticker mused. "Let's just say," he added, "that Madam Montfalcon don't know the half of what Mother Bessamy is or ain't. And she might do well to respect what she don't know, rather than try to knock it down."

"Geraldine doesn't respect anyone!" Tom answered. "She's awful to us and she says dreadful things about all of you! I hate her!"

There was a pause and a sigh before Pigsticker spoke.

"Master Thomas," he said, weighing his words with evident care, "don't you go hating, for hate is the root of all the dark trouble that's coming to this land, and coming swiftly it is. Hate is a kind of rot, that takes all the life out of things and turns them into dust. Some people, like that Miss Geraldine, they can't bear for others to be different, but that is nothing but fear; they fears that different means special, and themselves left out of it. Pity that kind, Master Thomas, rather than hating, for 'tis a terrible burden they bear."

"Hmm," said Tom, the words reminding him of Reverend Pilcher's preaching, which he had sat through on the odd Sunday when Father had remembered to send the boys off to his church. "But," he protested, "it's a bit hard to pity someone who puts nettles in your bed, when you get stings all over your ankle."

Pigsticker saw the justice of that and did not argue. It was Gilbert who spoke up.

"I have given some thought to that," he said, in his careful way, "and there is a fault in our reasoning. I awoke with the stings on the very day on which Geraldine visited the site. Therefore, even if she did place the nettles in the sheets, those nettles could not possibly have caused the stings, because the stings had already happened before they were placed there."

"But…" said Tom, confused, "that would mean that…" and he broke off, trying to work out what, indeed, it would mean.

Suddenly, unexpectedly, Pigsticker chortled.

"Like I says, Master Thomas," he said, "folks is different. Maybe some folks should put their boots on when they goes dreaming."

Though Tom was bursting to find out what this strange statement might mean, he had no chance to ask, because at that moment there was a flurry of wings and a black and white bird swooped down to land in a heap at Pigsticker's feet.

"Ah, Kapchak, good evening," said the old Gypsy, doffing his hat and holding out a knobbly finger.

The bird perched itself on the finger and let fly with a stream of loud, rapid-fire chatter. As Tom sat watching, open-mouthed, Pigsticker spoke seriously in reply.

"Kapchak," he said, 'I know you don't be liking her, but we needs to know where the young lady is right now, for it seems we must find her if things is to happen in their proper time this night."

The magpie croaked harshly twice, its beak opening and shutting like a rusty trap. Then it uttered some more staccato chatter, a long burst followed by a shorter one. Pigsticker nodded gravely and thanked the magpie courteously, before lowering his finger to let him hop down to the ground.

"Kapchak says," began Pigsticker, not acknowledging the dumbstruck looks on Tom and Gilbert's faces, "that Miss Geraldine has gone into the woods a while since, and is trampling around making a noise like a dozen horses in the bracken. He has no idea what she's doing and he suggests that we leave her to get lost, but we needs her, so that we cannot do."

The bird made a distinctly rude sound and began to preen its breast feathers, grumbling to itself and scratching irritably with its long, black claws.

"Why would Geraldine have gone into the woods?" asked Tom, "I thought she'd be swanning round the village, showing off. I can't see why she'd go there, away from her audience, all on her own…"

"I think she wishes to see the Gypsy festival," Gilbert said, matter-of-factly, "because she showed an interest in it when I met her at the pageant. She had the magpie with her then. She said that it was just a nuisance and that it didn't know when it was not wanted, and…"

"Gil, stop!" said Tom, putting up his hand. Gilbert stopped. "What do you mean, she showed an interest in the Gypsy festival? Did you talk to her about it?" he asked, worried now because Willow's closed mouth had led him to believe that the festival was a private, maybe even secret, matter. Would Pigsticker be angry that Gilbert had talked of it?

"She asked me what they do, and where it takes place,"

Gilbert answered, "but of course, I could not tell her for certain, as I did not know myself."

"So now we knows, or leastways, we knows enough," Pigsticker declared, tapping out and pocketing his pipe in preparation for leaving. He didn't seem angry, only purposeful, and Tom was relieved.

"We must track her down, and she must return the stone," Pigsticker announced. "Master Thomas, Mister Gilbert, come with me. We will need to get a hurry on, for time is moving along."

At this, Kapchak launched himself into the air and Pigsticker hurried after him. Tom and Gilbert looked at each other for a moment, before getting up off the grass, quickly dousing the tiny fire, and scrambling after them. Gilbert's face was unreadable, but Tom's was alight with excitement.

At last! A real adventure!

CHAPTER 13

And so the hunt for Geraldine began. Kapchak led the way, sometimes flying, sometimes hopping and flapping along the ground. He appeared untroubled by the deepening darkness, as did Pigsticker, who kept up a brisk pace through the crackling bracken. Tom followed behind, trying to avoid the snagging clutch of brambles, ducking to avoid low branches and pushing back springy saplings as he went, doing his best not to let them whip back and strike Gilbert, who was toiling away behind him.

As the darkness pressed in all around, Tom had the impression that he was tunnelling ever deeper into the green heart of the wood. He lost all sense of direction and simply ploughed on, until he became aware that his brother had fallen far behind. For though Gilbert could trudge on doggedly all day, moving quickly was very much against his nature. Fearing that they might lose him, Tom put on a spurt of speed to catch up with Pigsticker and asked for a short rest.

Pigsticker agreed, though it was clear he would have preferred to press on. With a whistle and a word, he sent the tireless Kapchak ahead to continue the search for any sign of Geraldine. Catching up at last, Gilbert flopped against a tree, struggling for breath, a pained expression on his face. Pigsticker turned to the boys and when he spoke his voice was hushed and worried.

"'Tis a bad night for a gaujo to be loose in these woods, unknowing," he said. "Paths that's there on other days might be gone, and the landmarks all shifted and changed. The ways through the forest this night is the older, wilder ways, and them that is abroad must follow them; but those old pathways has a mind to go where they will, and they might just take you with them if you don't know how they goes…"

He looked at Tom and saw his eyes widen in the darkness.

"Don't you worry," he added, in a more reassuring tone, "old Kapchak and me, we's been here before, many's the time. We'll not lose our way, and we'll find that young madam before too long, I don't doubt."

As they waited for the magpie to return, Tom took the chance to ask a question which had been forming in his mind for a while.

"Pigsticker," he began, "you said that Kapchak had been keeping an eye on Geraldine for you. Am I allowed to ask, who's been keeping an eye on us? I think someone has, but I've never quite managed to catch sight of them, I just haven't ever been quick enough."

Pigsticker looked down at him and his teeth showed white as he grinned in the darkness.

"Ah," he said, scratching the back of his neck and looking rather uncomfortable, "you worked that out, did you? Well, fair's fair, I'll not hide from you, Master Thomas. I has had a good few eyes on you and Mister Gilbert, begging your pardon for it, and with no insult meant. Only what with you digging around by the Maidens, it looked like you might get muxed up in this business; so I showed you to the busies and they keeps their eyes on you – and has no easy job of it, let me tell you! They has needed their wings for keeping up with you, Master Thomas; but they has done it well, and done it gladly, too, for they finds you agreeable company. So there you has it."

But Tom remained mystified.

"The busies?" he asked. "Who are they? And what do you mean, you showed me to them?"

Pigsticker didn't answer, just waited, and in a few moments, Tom realised the truth.

"The bees!" he exclaimed. "When we went to get the honey!"

Pigsticker nodded.

"The *pishoms* is good watchers," he said, "even if they knows rather more than they lets on, as a rule."

Gilbert, still breathless, could not resist questioning this statement.

"Bees," he wheezed, "clearly lack… the power of speech. How is it possible… for an insect to report information, when it has… no means of producing words?"

Pigsticker had a ready response to this.

"The words of the bee-kind is in the dance," he said, "if you knows the way of it."

Gilbert was less than satisfied with this cryptic answer, but Tom knew better than to let him start on a scientific enquiry which might take all night.

"I'm surprised about the bees," he quickly said to Pigsticker, "I thought it might be the badger."

Pigsticker gave a snort of laughter.

"Badgers!" he exclaimed. "They is a funny lot. You never can tell with badgers."

At this point, a scuffling rustle of wings and leaves announced the return of the magpie, who landed messily on a branch above Pigsticker's head. This time the rattling chatter of the bird was more muted, and went on for a little longer than before. Pigsticker listened intently, and when Kapchak fell silent, the old man pushed his hat to the back of his head and ran a hand through his hair in a distracted kind of way.

"What did he say?" asked Tom, urgently, catching Pigsticker's mood as the bird on the branch cawed one more time, a grim sound.

"Let's just say this, Master Thomas, Mister Gilbert; I had hoped for better news. We must be on our way, and lose no time, if this night is to be saved."

And with that, he pulled his hat back down into place and he was off again, moving in his fleet-footed way, finding the dark paths between the trees, and Tom and Gilbert followed as best they could.

This time the pace was relentless. Forced now to run so as not to lose sight of Pigsticker's back, Tom felt that he was moving through a blur of hazy darkness, with the sound of his own breath loud in his ears. Every time his feet hit the ground, whether on the soft leaf litter or the hard roots of trees, he felt the earth pulse in reply, echoing his own urgent heartbeat. He could distantly hear Gilbert crashing along behind him but knew that, whatever happened, he could not stop running if he tried. He felt like a twig in a fast-running stream, being pulled ever onwards to who-knows-where.

Then, suddenly, Pigsticker slowed right down and halted, making a drawn-out 'whoa' sound like a ploughman might make to his horse. The boys stumbled gratefully to a stop, then stood together, panting heavily, unable to speak. Pigsticker motioned them to stay quiet, then pointed up ahead and stood listening for a short time. He seemed hardly to have noticed the run, despite his age, and he breathed easily, unruffled. The magpie perched on his shoulder and the two of them conferred.

When agreement was reached, the bird flew off again. Pigsticker turned to Tom and Gilbert and spoke in the same low voice as before.

"Not far to go now," he said, "just past that stand of young oaks – Old Kapchak's gone ahead and we shall go after. Stay close now, and we'll see what we has found."

So they edged through the close-growing bushes and trees, peering into the dark and straining to hear. Soon, even Tom and Gilbert could pick out the flickering of lights through the branches, and hear what were definitely human voices.

"That's Geraldine!" exclaimed Tom in an excited whisper, when they got close enough to hear more clearly. Actually, there was no need to be particularly close, as the girl's voice now rose to almost screaming pitch.

"Leave me alone!" she shouted, fury and fear mingling in her voice. "Get off me! Get off, let me go!"

She seemed to be struggling, and Pigsticker leapt into a run again, towards the urgent sound and the lights. Tom followed quickly, frowning and worried, and Gilbert lumbered along after him. They covered the last few yards in a scrambling gallop and broke out from among the young oaks into a small grassy space. There, they saw that the light was the orange glow of flames.

The flames were those of two fire torches, suddenly bright after the darkness of the wood. They revealed the sight of Geraldine, struggling and protesting for all she was worth, being firmly held by the wrists by two smallish, dark figures. Tom stopped in his tracks at the sight: grey fur, dark faces peering out from under shadowing hoods… it was just as he had seen them in his dream, though more real than he could ever have believed.

Geraldine, for her part, was shocked at the sound and sight of Pigsticker and the boys crashing through the trees into the clearing. The fear on her face, however, quickly turned to something approaching relief – then to indignation.

"At last!" she burst out. "Someone who speaks English! Get these animals off me, will you?"

She continued to jerk and tug with her arms to try to get free, though she could not prise herself out the grip of the figures in grey.

Pigsticker took command of the situation. Stepping closer into the circle of torchlight, he stood, unafraid, until the struggling stopped. As all eyes turned to him and silence fell, he spoke in a strong, clear voice. The words made the hair stand up on the back of Tom's neck and his mouth drop open in surprise. For Pigsticker's words were not English, nor yet Romany, but a harsh yet lilting language, which Tom had heard before only within his own head and his own dreams.

The speech was short. Tom and Geraldine did not understand a word, but Geraldine's captors reluctantly released her, then stood beside her, waiting to speak. Now that he had a chance to see them better, Tom saw that they were a young man, much the same age as Gilbert, and a woman, who carried a long knife at her side and appeared strong and fierce, for all that she was barely as tall as Geraldine. They were wearing grey cloaks kilted up through heavy belts, with some kind of tunics and leggings beneath. The woman's hood was trimmed with grey fur, and she wore a necklace that looked to be made from shards of bone, or maybe teeth.

It was the woman who replied to Pigsticker, again, in the half-Welsh language which he had used. In her voice it sounded even more outlandish, and she seemed from her tone and gestures to be justifying her treatment of Geraldine. The young man stood by, holding his torch in one hand and using the other to stroke the hilt of a dagger which was tucked into his belt. Tom held his breath and felt his fingers cross again, though what he was hoping for, he wasn't sure. He flinched as Kapchak fluttered onto his shoulder. Then he and the bird stood, staring, waiting for whatever would happen next.

Meanwhile, Gilbert was listening intently to the language being spoken. Ignoring the bizarre scene in front of him, he closed his eyes and concentrated on tuning his ear to the strange sounds and words. He, too, had heard them before, only a few nights ago. In an undertone, he repeated and translated snippets, frowning deeply with effort and often correcting himself as he went along. Tom was torn between trying to listen to his brother and watching the scene in front of him, open-mouthed.

It was clear that the warlike strangers recognised some kind of authority in Pigsticker, for they spoke to him with some respect. Tom longed to know what they were saying. Trying not to draw attention to himself by making a sound, he edged closer to his brother.

"Blessed Earth," Gilbert was muttering, "had that before… *troseddu*, sounds like, *troseddu*, trespass… stars again, *seren*, stars… sounds like *ymwthiad*… intrusion, intruder…" Tom, desperate to understand, risked interrupting him.

"Gil!" he hissed. "What are they saying?"

"As far as I can tell, Thomas," Gilbert replied, his eyes screwed up with concentration, "they are saying that Geraldine is an intruder here and not welcome, though that seems evident from their manhandling of her. More about the Earth and stars, and as before, talk of the time coming close. More than that, I cannot say, and now I have lost my place."

But it seemed that the discussion was at a close anyway. Tom was uncertain what had been agreed, but something had, and Pigsticker motioned to him and Gilbert to follow him again. So the party moved off, Geraldine's captors leading, followed by Geraldine and Pigsticker, with the boys and Kapchak bringing up the rear.

As they walked, the old Gypsy turned to them to offer at least a partial explanation.

"Sorry, Master Thomas, Mister Gilbert," he said, "I had to set a few things straight there and no time for telling it twice. These here is warriors and they's pretty sharp if they thinks the King's under threat."

But before he could go any further, Geraldine interrupted him. She was walking unwillingly along, white-faced and rubbing her reddened wrists.

"I don't even know their stupid king," she said, angry

and close to tears, "I insist that you escort me back to the village right now!"

Pigsticker bristled visibly. When he spoke, his voice was dangerously quiet and controlled.

"Now listen here, Miss Montfalcon," he said, "this trouble you has brought upon yourself, and high-and-mighty talking ain't the way to get out of it. You has put a lot at risk with your thieving and meddling, and much has to be done to save this night."

Geraldine opened her mouth to reply, but before she could say a word, Pigsticker gestured towards the two grey figures ahead, moving smoothly and surely through the trees with their torches aloft.

"See them?" he said, "Them there has no cause to care if you is the squire's daughter or the Duchess of Devonshire – they will do their duty as they sees fit. So the best thing you can do, Missy, is keep quiet, do as you're told and let us try to put this matter to rights, before it's too late for us all."

He finished with a decisive nod and for once, Geraldine was left speechless. So she simply shrugged the strap of her camera case higher onto her shoulder, huffed an angry sigh, and then lapsed into sulky silence.

"Like I says, Master Thomas, Mr Gilbert," Pigsticker continued in his normal voice, as they marched on, following the light of the torches, "these is the King's warriors, his guards, or some of them at least. It is their task to see that no harm comes to the King, and a long time they has been about it, down through more years than anyone can reckon. More of them is waiting a half-mile distant, and we shall meet their leader there and take steps to put this business to rights."

"What will they do to us?" asked Tom, struggling to copy the old man's calm.

Pigsticker looked sideways at him as they walked.

"To see the Finders..." he began thoughtfully, "that is an honour to them, in no small way. By rights, they should offer homage. But now, the Queen has been touched by an unchosen hand, and there is no saying what might follow from that."

Here, Pigsticker looked pointedly at Geraldine, who huffed in response.

Don't look at me like that, old man. None of this is my fault. So just stop it!

Tom tried to change the direction of the conversation.

"Pigsticker, may I ask, what king do you mean?" he inquired, "I don't think you mean Edward VII do you?'

But the only answer the old Gypsy had for him was, "Think back, Master Thomas; for you has heard of him before."

And with that he fell silent, leaving Tom to wonder and Gilbert to frown in confusion as they marched on through the wood.

It was, as Pigsticker had said, about half a mile's march from the small clearing by the oaks to where the warlike strangers were leading the small party. It was easier walking with the light of the torches up ahead, though Geraldine's buttoned boots were not made for rough terrain and her feet were becoming sore and blistered. Though she tried to hide it, she was often startled, when the leaping flames of the torches made shadows suddenly rise up, as if to grab her from among the trees.

Noting her nervousness, Tom found that he himself was feeling unusually alert and really rather peculiar, just as he had the last time he had walked through the forest by torchlight. That night he had sensed that there was something oddly alive and vibrant about the wood, and had felt a wild kind of energy that seemed to come from the Earth itself. Now, that feeling was upon him again, though with an added sense of danger from the sight of the armed strangers who led the way.

Was it one of these people I saw in the wood that night? When Pigsticker said I didn't? Why would he say that?

The young warrior who was leading the way also seemed edgy. He often looked back at his former captive and her strange companions, as if he could not quite believe what he was seeing. His narrow, dark face was full of curiosity. Catching his eye, Tom dared a half-smile, which the young man returned before quickly turning stern and looking ahead again. The older female warrior put her hand on his shoulder and spoke to him quietly in their own language, and the youngster did not look round again. So they walked on, nobody speaking, each member of the unlikely procession wrapped in his or her own thoughts.

Ninety-seven, ninety-eight, ninety-nine, one hundred. And one, two, three, four, five, six, seven, eight...

Oh, for heaven's sake. What on Earth is going on here? I hate this. This is not funny. Something is seriously wrong with all of this. I wish I'd never come to this stupid wood. Those... those animals, those savages... who on Earth are they? They don't even seem real, they belong in some stupid story. They should be rounded up, they're a danger to normal people... Oh, God, I think they mean to kill us all.

I can't believe this, cannot believe it at all! I hope Gil's all right – he looks like he's counting steps – that'll calm him down. Oh, my... Oh! This is so exciting!

Soon after this, the warrior woman gestured to the young man and he ran on ahead. Tom and his companions watched the bobbing light of his single torch shrink away and disappear among the trees. After a time, they reached a clearing between some tall, old oaks. There the young man stood, his single torch now joined by several others, at the front of a group of about three dozen of the dark warrior figures. Some waited with weapons drawn, facing the oncoming strangers menacingly. They were flanked by riders on small, sturdy horses which snorted and fidgeted, ready to charge, just awaiting the command.

Seeing them all there, Tom's heart thumped and the hair stood up on the back of his neck, spreading a shiver right down his spine. He almost stopped walking, but Pigsticker urged him on and Kapchak dug his claws into Tom's shoulder like spurs. So he took a deep breath and walked on, and Gilbert stayed alongside him, though his hands had begun to flap at his sides and his breath was rough and fearful. Geraldine tried to edge behind Pigsticker, but to no avail. Before any of the three felt anything like ready, they were brought face to face with the mysterious King's guards.

CHAPTER 14

Time stood still for several seconds. There in the clearing, flickering torches lit a scene from legend, or from a distant, half-imagined past. Tom stared, wide-eyed, while dreamlike images of that time played across his mind, vivid and stark. Pictures of an era of tribal living and brutal warfare, when hunters ran down game from horseback, when firelit feasts were held in halls of timber and thatch, and when no churches stood on the rugged, untamed land.

Torches crackled and spluttered, the smoky scent of them flavouring the air. The small, tough horses stamped and snorted in their restlessness, while firelight glinted on the metal of swords and knives. Tom felt waves of thrilling fear running through him and his fingers crossed ever more tightly. Gilbert stood at his brother's side, his hands flapping and twitching as he worked hard to control his urge to run. Geraldine simply looked shocked to her very soul.

Then, with neither word nor warning, the small crowd parted down the centre, and a single figure emerged and strode forward. A leader, clearly, moving with an authority that none would question. He was taller than his fellows and his grey cloak had an elaborate hood, cleverly fashioned from the pelt of a badger. Tom noted the black and white stripes and a set of menacing teeth, and saw that when it was pulled down low over the wearer's forehead, as now, it gave the impression that the animal itself was alive and speaking.

The voice that emerged from the shadow of the badger hood was clear and strong, and once again, Tom was shocked by familiarity. It was the very voice from his dream, using again the half-Welsh language whose meaning he had felt rather than understood. The words he spoke were clearly a challenge. When he fell silent and stood before his people, waiting for a response, the air between the trees tingled and hummed with tension.

As before, Pigsticker stepped forward. When he spoke, there was both strength and weight in his words. It seemed that the old Gypsy greeted the leader of the warrior band with some respect, and he might have praised the two who had found Geraldine in the wood, as both stood a little straighter and it seemed that the young man was struggling to keep a grin off his face. Then Pigsticker walked up to the leader and clasped his arm. There was a heart-stopping pause as the man stood undecided, weighing up his response. Tom felt every muscle in his body tighten in desperate hope.

Please, please, please, please, please...

Then, decision made, the warrior chief returned Pigsticker's gesture. For a moment, the two stood facing each other, respect and strong hands holding them together. Suddenly it was as if everyone present could breathe again.

Pigsticker continued to talk. First, he pointed to Tom and Gilbert, and though neither knew the whole of what he was saying, they could read enough from his gestures and the odd word to understand that he was explaining about their finding of the stone. He pointed to the sky and then to Tom, and the leader at once turned and gave a short command to his warriors. All shifted to face Tom and Gilbert and, as one, made a brief gesture; a touch of the hand to the heart which was clearly a salute. Tom felt himself blush and, like the young warrior, he could barely keep the smile from his face.

But then the encounter took a troublesome turn, as the warrior leader pointed to Geraldine, and his voice and his hands asked about her part in the night's events. Pigsticker began to explain, and suddenly there was a change of mood among the gathered people. There were some shocked exclamations and much uneasy movement, many questioning looks and a general reaching for weapons. But the leader quietened them with an outstretched hand and gestured to Pigsticker to continue. He did, and after a further exchange, some agreement seemed to be reached, though nobody seemed completely at ease with it.

With all eyes watching them, Pigsticker turned to talk to Tom, Gilbert and Geraldine, while Kapchak stared right back at the warriors as if daring them to interrupt.

"Miss Montfalcon," Pigsticker said, "we knows that you has the stone, that you took it from Mister Gilbert's tent. If you would save your skin, you must tell us truthfully where you has put it, so that it can be brought back – for the time when it is needed is perilous close and its loss shall do more harm than you can know. Where is the stone?"

Geraldine lowered her eyes. She made no attempt to lie or deny.

"It's in my bedroom," she said.

"So now we knows," was Pigsticker's response.

He looked at Gilbert, who was silently shaking, his face white, and knew the deep horror and alarm that he was feeling.

"Don't you fear," he said to him, in his strong, calm, voice, "we shall bring her back. Master Thomas, can you ride?"

"Erm… I can, but I haven't for a while," he replied honestly.

Can I ride? What on Earth is he thinking of?

"Good," said Pigsticker, "for that helps the makings of a plan which I reckon might give us a fighting chance. I shall tell these here that we can fetch the stone, and try to make out that it was took by mistake and has been in safekeeping. But it must be you, Master Thomas, as fetches it."

"Me?" gasped Tom. "Why me?"

Pigsticker gestured carefully.

"These here won't let the young miss out of their sight," he said, "not being sure yet if she has done for this whole night. I can set you on the right way to the squire's house, but getting to the stone might be tricky. I reckon you'd be in least trouble should you be found in there, you being a friend and all." (Here he winked meaningfully). "As well as that, you could fit in through that window round the back that don't shut properly, though be careful for 'tis in view of the stables."

"How do you know…?" Geraldine began indignantly, but a sharp look from Pigsticker quickly silenced her.

"Bring the stone back, quick as quick, and we may just be right," he finished. Tom nodded, speechless.

And so the plan was made, and Pigsticker went to propose it to the warrior leader. He accepted it, though warily, and insisting that Geraldine remain in his sight. A pony was readied for Tom, and another for the young warrior whom Pigsticker had praised. He would go with Tom to guard his mount while he was inside. Tom took a moment to speak to Gilbert, encouraging him to remain calm and assuring him that Pigsticker would be there with him throughout.

"I think, Thomas," said Gilbert seriously, "that this plan is fraught with danger. Firstly, there is the matter of navigation; it is difficult to find ways through this forest in the dark and our present location is unknown. Secondly, there is the matter of crossing the common between the forest and the mansion; there are many rabbit holes which might cause a horse to stumble and fall. Then there is the risk of being found inside the house without permission, which might be seen as trespassing, which is against the law. I fear that this venture could end in disaster."

"Oh, do be quiet, for heaven's sake!" Geraldine exclaimed, disgustedly, cutting in on the gloomy monologue.

"Tom," she said, "simply do as you must and get the dratted stone back. It's on my dressing table, in my room, the first one at the top of the stairs. Father will still be out, probably searching for me like a demented... thing, but there are three servants who will be present, so do be quiet. *Do not get caught*, because I honestly think that these savages will roast me on a spit if they don't get their stupid stone. I wish I'd never set eyes on the thing. Just bring it back, and let me get out of here alive."

Then her voice lowered. "I know you don't like me," she said, seriously, "but there would be very serious trouble for you if you were involved in my... disappearance."

She swallowed hard with the effort of keeping up her bravado, and genuine fear showed in her eyes.

In spite of himself, Tom was moved.

"I'll do my best," he said.

Then it was time to go. The young warrior was already mounted on his pony, which was dancing and kicking up its back legs, eager to be off. Tom's mount was brought to him, a dark greyish roan with a black mane and tail, with a simple leather bridle and a sheepskin pad for a saddle. As Tom scrambled onto its back, Pigsticker stood by the horse's head, talking to it and stroking its velvety face. When he saw that Tom was mounted, he stepped round to speak to him.

"Take this," said the old Gypsy, pulling off his old felt hat and handing it to Tom. "Put the stone in it, for holding it can make a person dizzy if they has a feeling for it. Keep it tight in there, and you'll come to no harm." Remembering his own experience of this, Tom gratefully stuffed the hat in his belt.

"And have this too, to put in your pocket," Pigsticker said, passing a small object to him.

Tom was surprised to see that it was a little piece of bread. He looked bemused, and Pigsticker quickly and quietly explained.

"A charm against bad luck," he said, nodding slightly, "this will help see you right."

"Thank you," said Tom.

I hope it works. Gil's right, this plan is madness.

Preparations over, Tom took a deep breath, sat as squarely as he could in the unfamiliar saddle and shortened the reins, trying to get the feel of the way the lively little pony stood and moved.

"You shall have no trouble with this 'un," Pigsticker assured him, "for I has had a word in his ear. He knows where to go, and will come back as he is bidden. All you must do is hang on, and see that you bring back the stone before the stars start to rain."

Before what?

Before Tom could even start to ask what this meant, there was a great whooping from just behind him. In a blur of pounding hoofs and flying hair, the young warrior sped past on his pony. Tom's mount leapt after it as if it had been fired from a cannon. Tom jerked backwards and then lurched heavily forwards, grabbing the pony's coarse mane as the beast snatched the reins from his hand in its excitement. The watchers raised a shrill war cry to send the riders on their way. In moments, the torchlight was left behind and the horses charged wildly, terrifyingly, into the blackness of the woods.

The trees were a maze in the darkness. The ponies swerved and scrambled their way along a narrow path between the rough trunks and Tom sucked in his breath hard, trying to shrink inwards to avoid a fatal crash. First one way, then the other, the hurtling pony leaned at heart-stopping angles as it rounded the bends, following the flying hoofs of its companion up ahead. Tom wound his hands into the mane and tucked down low over the animal's straining neck, realising that an overhanging bough could club him to the ground at any moment.

Hold on, just hold on…

Tom's eyes began to stream as the night air rushed by, turning the world to a dark, streaky blur. The pony's muscles, hard as iron, bunched and pulsed as it forced its short legs to an insane speed, white drops of lathery foam flying from its mouth. Again, Tom was assailed by the feeling of being sucked into a tunnel, only this time, it was full of devilish turns and twists. The noise of the driving hoof beats sounded loud in his head. He struggled to gain a grasp of the reins with one hand, the leather feeling damp and slick from the sweat between his fingers.

Whoooaaargh!

At length, the trees began to thin out at the edge of the wood, and the bracken and brambles grew thicker on the ground, forcing the ponies' crazed chase to an end. They reluctantly slowed and came to a halt and Tom and the young warrior both slid to the ground. Tom's legs almost gave way under him, weak and shaky from trying to grip the pony's sides. Lacking words, the two young men grinned breathlessly at each other and nodded, exhilarated and proud. The ponies touched noses and told their own tales in great huffing snorts, while their rounded sides heaved in and out like bellows.

Once the riders were out from under the cover of the trees, they found that the light of the moon and stars was surprisingly bright, casting faint shadows onto the ground. Tom saw that the heavens, now darkest blue, were still lit by the vast new constellation. He pointed this out to his companion, who smiled and nodded and touched his hand to his heart in the same way as his people had in the clearing. Tom returned the gesture, which caused the young warrior to grin again. Then they walked on through the waist-high bracken with the ponies' reins draped loosely over their arms, the beasts following quietly, making the most of the moments of rest.

Soon the bracken gave way to short, springy grass and occasional gorse bushes, marking the edge of the common. Tom saw that they had emerged from the wood on the far side, away from the archaeological camp and closer to the Montfalcon mansion, and the orange glow of the village's bonfire was just visible in the dark distance.

How did we get here? I've been completely lost for so long now I didn't know where we'd end up. The village... it feels like it's in another world. And the pageant still going on like nothing was happening. I can't believe it.

After a few moments, the young warrior gathered himself and vaulted easily back onto his pony, ready to continue. The little animal pranced and shied, showing that it was full of energy once more and eager to be off. Tom remounted rather more gingerly on his still-shaky legs, and prepared to follow again. This time, he was ready when his mount sprang forward and he kept his seat as they gathered speed, passing swiftly from canter to gallop on the smoother ground of the common.

Soon, riding straight and fast in the starlight with the wind singing in his ears, Tom began to feel a strange sensation. He felt he was flying several inches above the ground, and, as if to prove this true, the pony was never troubled by the rabbit holes Gilbert had feared. Free now of the fear of crashing into the dark trees, Tom felt himself seized by a mad joy. Unable to contain himself, he let out a whoop of his own, a war cry that was almost a shriek.

Out in front, his companion heard him and turned his head to whoop back, his dark hair whipping across his face until he pushed it back with one hand, holding the reins in the other. Tom briefly envied his riding skills, especially when the cries excited both the horses and Tom's turned as skittish as its friend. Tom was again forced to grab the mane to stay in the saddle, as his pony leapt high over a gorse bush, almost throwing him into the air.

"Calm down, you!" he said to it in a frenzied whisper.

The pony paid no attention whatsoever, just carried on galloping at top speed, bringing Tom ever closer to Geraldine's home, closing the gap to a mere quarter-mile.

At last, the common land and fields began to blend into to the more sculpted landscape of the mansion's surrounds and the ponies once more slowed to a jog-trot. Only now did Tom remember his mission. His spirits plunged and he felt a strong, gripping pang of anxiety.

Oh, no. What am I doing here? How did I let them talk me into this? Breaking into a house! I've never done anything like that before... well, except for breaking out of school that time, and then I got caned! If I'm caught, we're all doomed. Thrown off the site, maybe even thrown into jail. There are the gates... oh no... But I have to do it, heaven knows what'll happen to Gilbert if I don't... and as for Geraldine...!

Swallowing hard to force down nausea, Tom dismounted. His companion quietly took both horses, ready to melt away into the darkness. Tom tried to hide his fear behind a brave smile, but the young man was not fooled and his dark, moon-shadowed face was all concern. Unable to explain, Tom just shrugged and looked helpless for a brief moment, but the young warrior understood. He laid a comforting hand on Tom's shoulder, and grasped Tom's own hand with his other. His skin was strangely cool in the mild night air, but his look was warm and encouraging. Tom took a deep breath and nodded.

Then each turned towards where he must go, one slipping into the shadows with his animals, one furtively creeping past the gates and towards the house, making for the back, where, he hoped with all his heart, the window would be open and he would find his way in.

Chapter 15

Seen from the outside, the Montfalcon mansion was a fine, imposing structure. Tom had seen it a few times before, mostly in the early days of the dig when his father had visited to make arrangements with Geraldine's father – 'the squire', as Pigsticker had called him. He knew the road that led to the house, and that it had been widened and had a new surface laid for Mr Montfalcon's car. But Tom had not been inside the house and the Professor had never bothered to describe the interior; he would never have noticed it.

Tom had pictured how Geraldine's home must look, imagining it to be rich and ornate, with luxurious carpets, gold-framed pictures, fine carved furniture and twinkling chandeliers. He had envied her once or twice, particularly when his tent had sprung a leak one rainy day and become rather chilly and damp. Now, zigzagging from shadow to shadow as he crossed the lawn, taking cover behind the impressive mature trees as he went, he had no desire to be inside the mansion. He would have given anything to be far, far away.

When he reached the back of the house, Tom saw that it looked nothing like the front. It was as if several smaller buildings had been cobbled together into one, and rooms seemed to jut out anywhere, making a muddle of nooks and corners. Light spilled out from one downstairs window, which he guessed might be the servants' sitting room. Tom pressed himself up against a tree close to the window, peering around, while he tried to work out how to cross in front of it and so reach the window which Pigsticker had said might be open.

I just have to run; there's no other way...

Crossing his fingers tightly and taking a deep breath, Tom took his courage in both hands and dashed from his hiding place. He flattened himself against the wall of the house, panting. From there he could duck down and creep under the lit window without being seen. Scuttling along, bent double, with one foot in a flower border and one on the path, he passed under the window ledge, and caught the hum of voices inside.

Please don't look out, please don't look out! How many servants did she say? Two? Three? Can't remember. Window. There. Please be open. Please be open...

When he reached the window that was his goal, Tom felt a pang of despair, for it looked to be firmly closed. He also saw in that moment what Pigsticker had meant about it being visible from the stables, which were off to the right-hand side. Tom hoped that Mr Montfalcon's hunter would not sense the presence of an unfamiliar person and raise a racket, for it would surely alert the stable boy or any other servant nearby.

Tom turned to the window again, desperately searching for a way to prise it open. It was of the casement type, made of solid wood, and though it looked well worn it was strong and unyielding. His heart pounding and his palms sweating, Tom worked his fingernails into the tiny gap round the edge of the frame and tried to ease it open.

Though it felt as if it would pull his nails out, he kept going, willing it to budge, and finally, finally, he felt it give. He gave a firmer pull and the window gave up its resistance, swinging open like a small door in the wall.

Thank goodness for that!

There remained the task of climbing in; not easy, for the window was placed at about shoulder height. Tom grasped the sill with both hands, started himself off with a jump, then pulled with his arms. He scuffed at the wall with the toes of his boots to heave himself, inch by inch, through the gap. Bracing his knees against the hard ledge, he peered into the dark interior and eased gingerly forwards. Finally, he crawled onto what turned out to be a wooden draining board next to a large, square sink. Carefully, quietly, he reached round and closed the window behind him. Then, stretching out a cautious hand in front, he climbed warily down, to stand on a bare stone floor.

Thank heavens for lucifers...

Tom peered around soundlessly in the shadowy darkness, feeling in his pocket for a match. As quietly as he could, he took one out, lit it and held it up. In the brief flare of light he saw that he was in a kind of scullery. He spotted the door, then made his way to it on shaky tiptoe. The door latch clicked loudly under his nervous fingers and he froze for a horrible second. It took all of his nerve to push the door open and make his way into the interior of the Montfalcon family home.

First, Tom passed into a large, disorderly kitchen, dimly lit but thankfully deserted. A kettle on the stove gave out wisps of steam, suggesting that someone had been in the room not long before. Tom flitted through the kitchen as quickly as he dared and crept out into a tiny hallway, where a servants' staircase led up into the main part of the house. He paused for a moment at the foot of the narrow stairs and decided to take off his boots, his stockinged feet being so much quieter. He tied the laces together and hung the boots around his neck.

Heaven help me, I look like a burglar...

Soft-footed as a cat, Tom padded up the stairs and came to the main hallway of the house. Oil lamps on the wall were alight but turned down low – Tom realised that this would be to welcome the master of the house, probably expected home any time now. But even as he felt a brief panic at this thought, Tom couldn't help but notice the sad state of the hall. In the soft light of the lamps it looked unkempt and cluttered, rather than elegant and spacious as he had expected. An uncomfortable air, aloof yet forlorn, seemed to linger around it and it felt nothing like a home should feel.

Creeping along, Tom found his attention constantly drawn to the shadows on the walls and the bare wooden floor. The dark shapes of tea chests and packing crates lurked like misshapen bodies. Rolled-up carpets and upturned furniture, carelessly propped against them, gave them long, reaching limbs and blunt, headless necks. Worse were the stuffed and mounted animal heads which stared blindly from the walls. Far from looking like proud and valued trophies, they were merely moth-eaten relics of a grandeur long passed away, awaiting the mercy of being taken down and burnt. Tom shivered.

This place is horrible. Just get the stone, and get out.

Grimly, Tom made his cautious way between the

shadows, trying not to look at them, and arrived at the foot of the broad staircase that would take him to Geraldine's room. The carved wood of the balustrade was dusty and scabbed and various objects littered the stairs, ready to trip the unwary: discarded boots, paint pots, one or two books. Though there was carpet on the stairs, held by brass rods, it was rather flattened and shabby. The whole effect was of a space that was downtrodden and somehow unloved; a place to pass through without lingering.

To his dismay, Tom saw that the light from the lamps only seemed to reach about halfway up the stairs. He gulped, seeing that he would move into much deeper darkness at that point. But there was no choice but to press on, so he set a tentative foot on the bottom stair and began to creep upwards. Torn between the twin demands of speed and silence, his every nerve prickled and his heart thudded like a drum.

There it is… the first room at the top of the stairs… that's the one…

Peering through the gloom, Tom could see that the door to Geraldine's room was ornate and heavy, made of dark wood with a large black handle in a fancy design. He stepped warily towards it, but to his horror, the floor of the landing protested under his weight by giving a great, creaking groan. In the silent house, the sound was shockingly loud and Tom bit his bottom lip hard and screwed up his eyes.

Oh no! Oh help. Someone must have heard that.

In a sudden moment of decision, he scurried across the rest of the landing and squeezed into Geraldine's room, barely opening the door for fear of more creaking. Then he stood with his back pressed against the solid wood, trying to calm his racing heart and straining to listen for footsteps coming up the stairs.

Moonlight shone into Geraldine's room through a triple window, the curtains being only partially drawn. Tendrils of some twisted creeper were outlined across the glass like thin, witchy fingers. The dim, silvery light spilled across the wooden floor and over the rugs and the large bed, reducing the contents of the room to a colourless confusion.

I can't see a thing in here!

Tom briefly toyed with lighting a candle end, fingering through his pocket to check that he had one – yes, there it was, tangled in a string of sugar beads. But he decided not to, just in case the light might be seen under the door if a servant did come looking. So he was forced to walk slowly around with his hands out in front like a blind man, feeling his way along. His hand passed over the huge, carved bedstead and then to a hatstand. Something slippery slid from it onto his arm with a soft, hissing whisper. Tom flinched.

Aargh! Snake! No, fool. Just clothes. Settle down.

Shuddering, he pressed on through the half-dark. He eased past a school-style desk and chair, loaded with books in unsteady piles. There was the dressing table – tucked into an alcove, right across the large room, as far from the door as it could be.

Don't creak, floor, please don't creak…

Geraldine's room seemed to be half nursery, half lady's boudoir, and it was packed with possessions and surprisingly untidy. A large rocking horse stood in one corner, a picture hat perched at an angle on its head. Straining his eyes to see into the darker areas of the room, Tom was horrified when two dark eyes stared back at him from a white face on the wall – a puppet, hanging from the picture rail as if strung on the gibbet. Tom quickly turned his face away and marvelled instead at the size of Geraldine's wardrobe. A vast, polished-wood monster, it could have held enough clothing for a queen and all her ladies.

Finally, Tom came to the dressing table. He caught sight of his reflection in the mirror there; a ghostly, dishevelled figure, moving with exaggerated care, topped by a pale, worried face. He ignored it as best he could and scanned the table, searching among the bottles and powder puffs, paperweights, figurines, vases, framed pictures, silver hairbrushes, hand mirrors, hatpins and hairpins for the familiar shape of Gilbert's stone.

Finally, he spotted it, there among the feminine clutter. It lay uncomfortably next to a peacock-feather plume in a silver inkstand, half-buried under a lacy handkerchief. Remembering to cover his hand with Pigsticker's old hat, Tom reached carefully for the stone, almost as if it might burn him on contact. His hand closed around it and he felt the familiar, profound weight settle itself slightly, almost as if it wanted to be there.

Got it!

Tom took a second to close his eyes and let out his breath in a muted sigh of relief. But a moment later, as he turned to make his way from the dressing table to the door, disaster struck. Suddenly, his toe collided hard with something heavy made of metal – a fancy wrought-iron side table which he had not noticed in the gloom, and on it, a small water jug and a glass. With a crash and a splash, the whole thing tumbled down, the glass breaking and the table clanging hollowly against the wooden floorboards.

No! No, no, no, no, no!

Agonised, Tom scuttled to the window, seeking a route for an emergency escape. Yes, there were strong branches of creeper that looked serviceable, but it was no good, he could not get the window catch to open. His fumbling fingers suddenly seemed to be made of rubber yet as heavy as lead. Worse, he heard footsteps coming up the stairs and a definite sound of voices. With nowhere else to go, he held onto the stone, wrenched open the wardrobe door and squeezed in, just managing to get it shut as the door of the bedroom slowly opened.

Frozen by fear, Tom stood among a crush of fabrics and furs. His fingers tightly crossed themselves and he held on tight to the scrap of bread that Pigsticker had given him. He fought hard to quiet his breathing, while his throbbing toe pressed painfully against a knobbly buttoned boot. The wardrobe door muffled the sounds from outside, but still, he could make out that at least two people had come onto the landing and were now standing just inside the bedroom, talking in the high-pitched voices of frightened women.

"Ooh, I hate it here," squeaked one of them, "it gives me the horrors. All these bumps and creaks and Lord-knows-what, I swear it's haunted, I do!"

"Hush!" the other replied, fearfully, "I can't bear ghosties and devils and all that talk. I never heard no crash anyway."

"Well I did," came the first voice, shakily, "just like before. I'm sure there is something there."

"Well, you can go in and look if you're of a mind," said the other, "for I shan't. Oh, I wish the mistress'd come home. It don't seem so 'orrible when she's about."

"I'm not going in there!" gasped the first voice, "and I don't care what old Mrs B says. Listen, you tell her we looked and nothing doing, I must have imagined it, and I'll agree. How about that?"

"Fine," came the second voice, "now, let us be gone!"

This suggestion was clearly taken up, as rapid footsteps then descended the stairs, taking the voices with them.

Thank the stars for that. That was close!

After a few moments' pause, Tom eased himself stiffly out of the wardrobe. There was no way that he could make his way back through the house now that the servants were alerted; he would simply have to trust the creeper. He placed the heavy stone carefully inside his shirt to free both hands for climbing and slipped his boots back on. Then, before he could think too much about how high up he was, he forced the stubborn window open and climbed out. Hooking both feet into the creeper and testing it for strength, he finally let go of the window ledge and trusted his whole weight to the plant.

Hand over hand, feet feeling for firm holds, Tom began to climb downwards. The tangled creeper felt wiry and tough in his fingers, rather like a fishing net might feel, but it gave alarmingly at every move. His heart lurching, Tom scrabbled, swung and half-slid down the wall of the house, sometimes dangling for several seconds as his hands grappled for the stronger tendrils. He grated his skin on the older, woody stems and twice snagged his shirt on nails that stuck out from the wall. It was the most breathless, uncomfortable climb of his life.

Finally, Tom judged that he was close enough to the ground to risk letting go of the creeper. The baked earth slammed hard into his heels as he landed, shooting pain up into his ankles and calves. Wincing, he looked around wildly to see where he was and which way to run. He quickly got his bearings and set off at a staggering gallop towards where his companion would be waiting, trusting to the darkness to keep him hidden.

Then, all at once, a sound came through the night air that propelled him to even greater effort, though he felt as if his heart might burst.

Oh no! Mr Montfalcon!

Geraldine's father's car was roaring towards the house, its engine sound louder and higher than usual, suggesting that it was moving at considerable speed. Yes, there were its lights, two spots of white in the darkness, snaking fast along the road, taking the route that led to the back of the house.

Good… he won't have seen the horses… but God help me if he finds me here, escaping with stolen property!

Desperate to be far away, Tom ran as if the devil itself were on his tail.

When he passed the gates of the Montfalcon mansion, breathless and light-headed, Tom was momentarily lost in the darkness. His companion and the ponies were nowhere to be seen. He stopped and just stood for a few seconds, suddenly uncertain. He was about to call cautiously out, but before he did, he looked one more time into the wooded darkness. There, right in front of him, the young warrior stood, so still and quiet that Tom had missed him completely. Realising that he had been spotted, he stepped forward, making an inquiring gesture with his hand.

"I have it!" Tom said, breathlessly, and patted the bulge in his shirt.

The warrior raised his fist triumphantly and gave Tom a congratulatory slap on the shoulder that almost sent him sprawling. Then he took the reins of his fiery little horse and swung up onto its back, ready to leave. Tom saw his own pony waiting quietly and did the same, patting it profusely before he set off, regarding it now as a friend and ally. In seconds, they were gone from the place, the ponies' hoofs kicking up dust from the ground as, once more, they galloped away.

If the first ride had felt all too real at times, the return was entirely dreamlike. It seemed to Tom that mere moments passed in each stage of the ride – the parkland, the common, the tall, deep bracken, the twisty path through the pitch-dark woods – and yet each moment seemed to last an age. It was as if time had somehow slipped from its moorings and was flowing freely to a rhythm of its own. Tom lost himself in the thrill of speed, and felt none of the fear that had gripped him on the perilous ride out.

How could carrying a heavy stone make your body feel so light and wonderfully alive? How could the night air suddenly taste so sweet and fresh, and the moon shine so gloriously? And how could two galloping ponies go unnoticed when they thundered past within twenty yards of a group of villagers – even if they were returning home from a night of celebration and ale? Yet they did, and it was an experience that would live ever after in Tom's memory, and to which he would frequently return, both dreaming and awake – for it would never lose its savour, even after many years had passed.

CHAPTER 16

Tom and the warrior rode proudly back into the woodland, expecting a heroes' welcome. As the ponies drew to a sweaty, stamping halt, both youngsters called out in their own languages.

"We have it!"

But the words died away and no answering shouts came, either from the assembled ranks of warriors or from Tom's own companions. Though all eyes turned to the riders and there was a rustle of whispers, nobody moved to receive or congratulate them. The ponies stepped warily back, sniffing at the unease in the air. Tom felt all the joy of the wondrous ride ebb away, leaving him bewildered.

What's happened? Why does everyone look so grim? We got the stone back... surely all's well now?

He was relieved to see Pigsticker walk towards them, across the ring of torchlight – for though the old man's manner was not encouraging, he did at least seem to be about to speak, and hopefully, to explain.

Standing beside the ponies and their riders, Pigsticker spoke in English to Tom.

"You have played your part well," he said, "and must not fear that these doings are any fault of yours. Climb down, Master Thomas, and show them the stone, for the lost one is found again and your return may yet be timely."

Sliding off the pony, Tom speechlessly fished the hat

and its contents out of his shirt, while the young warrior also dismounted and led the beasts away, rejoining the silent ranks of his companions. They welcomed him with faint nods and brief greeting gestures.

"Hold it up, Master Thomas," said Pigsticker, indicating the stone.

Bemused, Tom did as he was asked. Without the hat for protection, the strange, half-metallic object quivered in his hand in a most peculiar way. As he stretched out his arm to hold up the stone, he suddenly felt as if it lifted itself and if he let it go it could fly right up to the heavens. He grasped it firmly and it settled in his fist, and all those who saw it drew in their breath in one long gasp. Many dropped to their knees, their hands to their hearts once again, their heads bowed in awe.

"Pigsticker," said Tom in an urgent whisper, as the moment stretched on, with no sign of what would happen next, "what's going on? What's wrong?"

Pigsticker pulled on his old hat and took a moment to settle it at the angle he preferred.

"To have the Queen back, that's to all our good," he said, seriously, "but She is only one part of this. She must be brought to the King when the stars is raining, for this is how it has always been. But the stars is not starting raining, as they should be, and the chief there," (here he gestured towards the warriors, now standing again, close together and stony-faced) "well, he has decided that young Miss Montfalcon has cursed this night with her meddling. He says she has stopped the stars coming down."

"What will he do?" Tom whispered back, with a worried frown.

"Well, er, mmm…" for once, Pigsticker seemed to be struggling for words. "Master Thomas," he said eventually, "you has to understand that you is dealing with different folks here, and different ways. These here warriors, they don't come under no laws of ours and they don't see things the same way we does. To them, the King is above everything and anyone that threatens Him, well, so much the worse for them. So he has taken the girl, and he has a mind to… well, to… erm, to…"

"To what?" asked Tom, alarmed now, for he had never seen Pigsticker look so uncomfortable.

"To maybe try and… well… shall we say… erm… lift her own curse… with her own… blood," he finished, unwillingly.

He pushed back his hat and ran a worried hand through his hair. Tom took a moment to register just what this might mean.

"He can't do that!" he exclaimed, "that would be…"

"Aye, it would be just that, to you or me or any judge in this land," Pigsticker cut in in a low and urgent voice, "but these here won't pay no heed to that, you can be sure of it. Now, I needs to go on talking with the chief, and you must see to Mister Gilbert, for he is beside himself. Take the stone to him, and help him back to his wits, for we has great need for some thinking here, and the more clear heads the better."

With that, Pigsticker turned away and walked back across the circle of torches to where the chief was waiting for him. As the warriors parted to let him through, Tom caught a chilling glimpse of Geraldine, alone among the fierce grey figures. She stood rigid and white-faced, too shocked and frightened even to protest. He meant to give her some kind of comforting or encouraging sign, but none came to him. Then the warriors' ranks quickly drew back together, and she was lost from sight.

Oh, no – that looks bad...

Tom found Gilbert on the edge of the clearing. He stood blank-faced, staring at nothing, rocking to and fro, but in a distracted, twitching way rather than in the rhythm that usually calmed his nerves. Words could not pierce that vacant staring, and in the end Tom had to resort to taking hold of his brother's hands (which he rarely did, as Gilbert usually didn't like being touched) and placing the stone between them. As it nestled in their joined hands, it gave off a strange, growing warmth, and finally, Gilbert looked down at Tom as if he had come back to himself.

Tom quickly explained what was happening, and Gilbert began in return to describe the scene when the warriors claimed Geraldine back, with warlike cries and weapons drawn.

"Gil," said Tom, stopping his brother's stream of words, "we have to think of something to get Geraldine back. We can't let her be..."

"A sacrifice, of a kind," Gilbert finished for him, "no. That would not do. And there is no need. An idea is coming to me, and it will take seven more minutes to work out the details. Will you ask Pigsticker to come over here, please? I will need him."

Tom knew that asking questions might make his

brother lose his train of thought altogether. So he simply nodded and turned away, leaving Gilbert talking softly to the stone in his hands.

How on Earth am I going to let them know I need to talk to Pigsticker? I don't know their language...

So, under the interested eyes of the warrior company, Tom sought out the young man who had ridden to the Montfalcon mansion with him. When he found him, he half asked, half acted out talking to the old man with the hat. The young man was initially mystified, but once he understood, he quickly relayed the message through the ranks. Before long, Tom was relieved to see Pigsticker emerge and walk over to him. He lost no time in passing on what Gilbert had said.

"I can't tell you any more than that, sorry," he said, but the Gypsy waved the apology away.

"Any ideas is welcome now," he said, "let's hear what the Finder has to say."

"Ah, Thomas, there you are," said Gilbert in a reassuringly normal tone of voice when Tom and Pigsticker appeared before him out of the torchlight. "Almost exactly seven minutes, to my reckoning, though I cannot say precisely, as my pocket watch has stopped, which is rather vexing. Usually it is highly reliable."

Tom bit back his impatience and forced himself not to interrupt.

"Mister Gilbert," Pigsticker said, gently but firmly, "what is the idea that you has? For we has a pressing need for a plan, once again, and time is against us."

Gilbert didn't seem to mind being prompted. Without further distractions, he began to explain his idea for the rescue of Geraldine. Tom listened carefully, and could not quite believe what he heard.

That's the last thing I would have expected from Gil! He's surprised me before, but never like this! But what if it doesn't work? It might save her, but it might make things worse... and there's no plan in there for how to get away if it all goes wrong... Oh, Gil, I hope you know what you're doing...

But with no better idea presenting itself, it was decided without argument that Gilbert's scheme would have to be tried.

The first part was left to Pigsticker. He was to go to the chief of the King's warriors and ask him to allow Gilbert to offer him a challenge. He, Pigsticker, would translate. Tom fretted horribly about the whole plan, though Gilbert, with the stone in his hand, seemed surprisingly calm and even quite content. He muttered thoughtfully to himself, preparing for his part, and once or twice asked Tom for advice about details. Tom, still not quite able to believe what was happening, tried to help him as best he could.

Meanwhile, the warriors remained eerily quiet. The only sounds in the dark wood were the rising and falling of voices, those of Pigsticker, the chief and one or two advisors, and the occasional huffing of a pony or thud of impatient hoofs on the ground. Tom screwed up his tired eyes and rubbed his face, taut from waiting. Anxiety was surging through him in nauseating waves.

I can't imagine what this must be like for Geraldine...

But soon the waiting was over, and this was almost worse, for now came the real test. Pigsticker emerged from the huddle of warriors and announced that their leader would indeed hear the challenge which Gilbert had suggested. He wished it to be known that neither he nor his people would shrink from any test of bravery or wits, nor ever had. So Pigsticker signalled to Gilbert, and with only the slightest hesitation, he stepped forward, out of the comforting gloom of the deep shadows and into the torchlit circle, before many watching eyes.

The warriors, in turn, parted their ranks to let the chief walk out and face the Finder. They brought Geraldine out under guard, shaky and pale with terror. Seeing Gilbert there did not fill her with any great confidence; she had not been included in any discussions about what was happening and could work out only that he was somehow to be her champion.

Oh, no. This is my saviour? Half-mad, tongue-tied, moonstruck Gilbert? What's he doing anyway, with his eyes shut and that cursed stone in his hand? I'm doomed.

Through the waiting silence, Gilbert finally spoke. He sounded steady and clear, and Tom was pleased to recognise his confident 'reciting' voice, the one he had used at the Gypsy campfire a lifetime, or perhaps a week, before.

"Warriors of the King!" Gilbert announced. "Justly are you famed for your skill with weapons and for your long devotion to your duty."

Through his desperate nervousness, Tom felt the faint twitch of a smile at this, for opening with praise had been his idea. Then Gilbert continued.

"I come before you with a challenge not of swords, but of words."

He must have got that from a story, I'm sure I've heard it before…

"I will ask you one riddle," Gilbert went on, "and should you prove unable to answer it correctly, the lady Geraldine must be returned to us, her honour restored."

Definitely from a story. He'd never use words like those. 'The lady Geraldine'?

At each stage of the speech, Gilbert halted, and Pigsticker translated for the assembled warriors. Tom watched their stony expressions change, first to looks of modest pleasure, then surprise and even outrage, and he crossed his fingers tightly, hoping that the battle to come really would be one of words only.

There was a pause. A hushed stillness descended, with even the horses standing motionless. Tom looked around at the scene before him: the ranks of grey-cloaked figures, the speakers standing alone, the prisoner held firm. To his overworked imagination, it looked rather like some strange and unknown chess game, the match half-finished, with one side standing strong and the other perilously close to defeat.

Perilous is right... there's hardly any chance of this working.

The torches still flickered, lighting the clearing with their orange flames and throwing jagged, smoky shadows. Above, the sky was now deepest black. Though the air was only just cool, Tom shivered and felt goosebumps spring up on his arms. The waiting seemed to go on forever.

When the chief finally spoke, the sound caught Tom by surprise. His heartbeat quickened and he pressed his crossed fingers together ever more tightly, waiting for Pigsticker to shape the words into English, so that he would know how the challenge had been received.

Pigsticker listened intently to the words, spoken out strongly and decisively from under the badger-striped hood. The old Gypsy nodded at times but continued to look serious, giving no real clues as to the decision being reached. Both Tom and Geraldine looked on, desperate to know what was being said, but Gilbert simply stood still, his eyes closed, silently mouthing words to himself. The sight gave Geraldine a further push towards despair; she felt her eyes grow hot and prickly and she fought to stem the rush of angry, frightened tears.

Gilbert... don't let me down, you, you... oh, God...

As Geraldine stood lost in her angry, fearful thoughts, the watching warriors listened approvingly to their leader's words ringing out. The Welsh-sounding syllables, rare and wild, remained a mystery to both Geraldine and Tom. Towards the end of the chief's quite lengthy speech, Pigsticker's expression grew more grave, and when he was finally able to start to translate, he blew out his cheeks in a gusty sigh.

"Well, that is as good as we are going to get," he said, "and it is some of what we hoped for. They will take your challenge, Mister Gilbert, and they have chosen not to ask a riddle of their own – them being masters of it, they says, and you not; that's to give you a chance, like, and good of them, you could say. But..." and here he paused and looked uncomfortably away from Geraldine's desperate eyes "... there's one thing he won't budge over, and you won't be liking it, I know..."

"What is it?" Tom asked in a strained whisper, finding that his voice would hardly work at all. "What did he say?"

"He says," Pigsticker began, "for the young lady to be

spared, he lays down two rules, not one. He shall let the young Miss go, but only if the riddle defeats him and his advisors, *and...*" Here Pigsticker stopped and scratched the side of his neck, most uncomfortably.

"And what?" Tom barely dared to whisper.

"And... if the Finder himself will stake his own life on her not having cursed this night..." Pigsticker's voice trailed away into silence.

"*His own life?*" Tom repeated, horrified. "What does he mean?"

One look at Pigsticker's face was enough to give Tom the dreadful answer.

"No!" he cried, shocked. "He can't do that! They can't ask that! Tell them, Pigsticker, that's not fair! Don't let them do anything to Gilbert!"

He ran out of words and stood, white-faced and shaking, more frightened than he had ever been in his life.

Gilbert's eyes opened and, when he spoke, it was in his usual matter-of-fact voice.

"How do they intend to verify that there has been no curse?" he asked. "What evidence would they require in order for the point to be proven?"

What! Gil, don't you understand? We're talking about life and death here – your life and death! Never mind evidence and all that! Wake up! This isn't a game!

Pigsticker seemed unsurprised by Gilbert's question, and answered him plainly.

"They will call it settled if, and only if, the stars starts to rain, like they should be already, but isn't," he explained. "And if they don't, he'll think it fit to take you, and Miss Montfalcon as well, for everything will be lost to them;

they will have failed in their duty, and will be out for blood in no small way."

Then he added:

"Like I says, Mr Gilbert, they lives by their own laws, and they is old laws, made only by themselves, and harsh, to our way of thinking."

"Oh," replied Gilbert simply, "I see. Then tell him, please, that we accept his terms."

"No, Gil, no!" protested Tom in anguish, unable to bear what he was hearing. "Don't do it! You can't! It's too dangerous, you're risking your life…" but here, his breath turned to a ragged sob and he gulped hard, unable to say anything more.

Geraldine, from her place under guard on the sidelines, said nothing. The tears which she had held back for so long broke through and ran in streams down her face. She swiped them angrily away with the heel of her hand and stood straight, trying to remain defiant in spite of everything. Gilbert looked across at her, then turned back to his brother.

"Thomas," he said, seriously, "we have no alternative plan which might prove better than this one."

And with that, Gilbert took his place before the ranks of warriors. Pigsticker translated his reply for the chief, and Gilbert closed his eyes again, ready to pose his riddle. Tom stood uncomfortably, hardly daring to watch, with his bruised toes crossed now as well as his fingers, and his heart firmly lodged in his mouth.

A hush settled over the clearing as Gilbert stepped forward. The waiting warriors looked on, wild and unearthly in the flaring torchlight. Geraldine stood staring, quivering with fear. Pigsticker placed himself between Gilbert and the chief, waiting to translate; his hat was pulled down low, hiding his face in shadow. With a gliding swoop, Kapchak flew down to perch on the old man's shoulder. Tom concentrated on breathing and tried to calm his racing heart.

After a long moment, Gilbert closed his eyes and, in the same reciting voice which he had used before, posed his riddle.

"What goes on four feet,

On two feet and three,

But the more feet it goes on

The weaker it be?"

The question hung in the air for a second before Pigsticker spoke it again, in the harshly musical sounds of the warriors' own tongue. It was greeted with murmurs and nods – a riddle well-asked, being heard with respect. Tom furrowed his brow.

I've heard that before, somewhere… please, please, don't let it be one they already know, please don't let them know it…

Gilbert stood with every appearance of calm, holding the stone in his cupped hands, while the warriors and their leader withdrew to discuss and confer.

Pigsticker watched the discussions between the chief and his people from his place near the centre of the clearing.

Aye, well, 'tis asked now and all is done that can be done. Now we shall see if these warriors' wits is as swift as their swords…

The hum of voices was too low for the Gypsy to

pick out the words, but the tone gave clues to what was happening. First the advisors spoke, then anyone from the company. It began with confident voices, seeming certain. Then, it seemed, various thoughtful suggestions were put forward. None seemed to be wholly right, and the spaces between suggestions grew longer and longer. It seemed that the warriors, wise as they might be, were at a loss.

Gradually the tone of the discussions began to change. The lack of answers sparked disagreement and then the exchange of heated words. But just as it seemed that swords might be drawn, they were halted by the strong, reasonable voice of the woman who had first found Geraldine in the wood. By the time she finished speaking, the talk had faded to a resigned murmur. Finally, the chief spoke to the warriors around him and his tone was wry, his gestures open-handed. He walked back towards Gilbert, and Pigsticker prepared to translate once again.

Tom understood no words of the chief's speech. But he could read his gestures and his stance, and he knew before Pigsticker confirmed it that no answer had been found. He whooped with joy and relief, then bounded joyfully over to congratulate his brother. Then he flung his arms round Pigsticker, (dislodging the squawking Kapchak) and leapt around in a war dance of pure excitement. The warriors watched him and, even in defeat, many of them were glad.

Gilbert smiled slightly and made to move away, back into the shadows. But at this, the chief's face turned to thunder and there was a sharp intake of breath from many of the watching warriors, which stopped Tom in his tracks.

"Gil!" he hissed to his brother. "Tell them the answer!"

"Oh yes," said Gilbert, as if the matter had slipped his mind. "The answer is 'Man.'"

Hurriedly, Pigsticker translated. The chief's expression turned to a slow, appreciative smile as full understanding dawned. He nodded and exchanged meaningful looks with his advisors. The moment of tension over, Tom made as if to return to his celebrating. But Gilbert and Pigsticker stood unmoved, and when Tom looked at Geraldine, still standing under guard, he halted suddenly. His heart sank, for only now did he remember the second condition of the challenge.

"Gil!" he gasped. "The stars. They have to start to rain, or…"

Gilbert simply pointed towards Pigsticker and the chief. Standing in the centre of the clearing, they were staring up into the sky. One by one, every person present joined them, and, at that moment, way up in the velvety darkness, one gleaming star gracefully fell. It drew a golden thread behind it, and, in the moments that followed, many others joined it, until the darkness was transformed to a dazzling shower of silver and gold.

"The Perseid meteor shower," said Gilbert, "is one of the more predictable occurrences in the astronomical year. I judged it due to begin at any time now, and I am pleased to have been proved correct."

Tom was speechless.

After this, several things happened in swift succession. Geraldine was released, and limped over to thank her saviour in halting words. Gilbert barely glanced at her, being thoroughly engrossed in the stone and the stars. There was some general milling around, some talking and shouting and laughter. A feeling of excitement and festivity began to break out. The young warrior who had ridden with Tom rushed happily over to him and clapped him heartily on the shoulder again. This time Tom managed to land a good, friendly slap of his own, and the two of them laughed together.

Pigsticker and the chief began to bring the company to order. There was a gathering of torches, hurried explanations and some jostling for position, until Tom found himself alongside his brother at the head of a kind of procession. Flanked by the chief and Pigsticker, with Kapchak flying ahead and the stars raining overhead, the Finders headed out of the clearing, taking the stone to where it needed to be. Finally, it seemed, its time had come.

CHAPTER 17

Was this another dream, or was it real? Tom walked proudly at the head of the procession through the wood, his senses more sharp and alive than they had ever been in his life. A broad, green path opened up in front of them, between the trees, inviting them ever deeper into the heart of the wood.

This is the stone's doing, I know it is – though I don't know how a rock, or metal or whatever it is, could have the power to do all this. I've dreamed of it, searched for it, felt it... even stolen it, and I still don't understand it. I just know this is the best adventure I could ever have wished for...

And now, riding in Gilbert's hands, the stone was finally going to meet its own destiny. It seemed to be silently singing of its joy and eagerness and longing. The feeling spread to the entire company and their excitement carried them along like a powerful tidal surge. Tom turned to grin at his brother, who was walking steadily, carrying the precious object with his usual serious care. For once, Gilbert looked back at him and smiled in return.

She is content now. Content to be going where she belongs. Content, but not quiet. Singing. A singing stone. There can be no such thing, and yet there is. This is all extremely pleasant.

Geraldine, following behind, had little idea what was

going on. She was simply relieved that the outrageous, fur-clad savages had finally let her go.

I shall stay close to Tom and Gilbert, for at least they come from a world which I believe actually exists – though heaven help us if those two stand for normality. And as for that old Gypsy… what is his part in all of this? He seems to know what's afoot. He is clearly involved with those wildlife-scented ruffians; old Badger-head there sees something in him that he respects. Even that scabby feather duster of a magpie seems to know what is happening, and have a part to play. Ow, my blisters! I wonder whether Tommy would carry this camera for me?

But she thought better of asking, and walked on, wincing.

Tom was now thoroughly enjoying himself. Looking back in wonder at the host of warriors and horses that followed him, he was delighted to see that their numbers were swelling. There were familiar faces among the growing crowd. There was Willow, graceful and exotic in velvet and gold; with her, Rosebay and Darkus, also in their finery and for once not arguing. An excited and round-eyed Cobby perched on Tinman's shoulders, and Magister the horse walked beside them, his mane and tail brushed to a rippling shine.

The procession continued to grow as they passed through the woods. Senso, the lurcher, stepped elegantly at his master's heel, ignoring Tinman's ferrets, who ran playfully between his legs. The old fiddler was there, looking well feasted and content, and, on his arm, a familiar elderly lady whose noisy terrier scurried and bounded alongside her. And still more joined the increasingly excited crowd, and the road seemed to broaden to accommodate them all, human and animal, Gypsy and warrior, Finders and companions, all following the stone.

But to where? Tom realised that he had no idea where the procession was bound. He turned to ask Pigsticker, who looked down at him from under the brim of his hat, his eyes twinkling.

"It's not so much where," he replied with a grin, "as who."

What does that mean? Pigsticker, I'll never understand all that you say.

Content to wait and see, Tom carried on walking, enjoying the lively, springy feeling of the ground under his feet. Everything in the wood seemed to be unusually full of life this night. Tom could have sworn that the trees leaned slightly forwards as the procession passed by, lowering their branches as if bowing to the stone.

Trees and animals and people and everything... everyone can feel it. This is wonderful.

Small, shy night creatures that would normally have scuttled away at the sound of so many feet sat inquisitively at the sides of the green road. Some even followed along, hopping and scurrying through the grass and ferns, adding their own tiny sounds to the cheerful hubbub. Badger and fox, hedgehog and mouse, and even a smooth green grass snake came along, while (to Geraldine's horror, and Tom's delight) moths whirred through the air and a barn owl spread its graceful wings to glide above them all.

Finally, Tom realised that their destination was in sight. The path gradually fanned out into a spacious clearing surrounded by vast and regal trees. The mood of the company changed as they drew near to it; where there had been chat and laughter, calling out and banter, neighing and snuffling in the ranks, now the tone became more hushed, more reverent. The feet that had swished freely through the summer grass slowed to a dignified pace and even the animals placed hoofs or paws with care.

This is like walking into a cathedral... like being out of the world, somehow... but more in it than ever... if that makes any sense at all...

Tom would have liked to share this observation with Gilbert, but he saw that his brother was utterly caught up in the stone. His eyes half-closed, he was whispering to it in Welsh, out of reach of any interruption. So instead, Tom stared up into the heavens, to where the trees' lofty branches held up a vast domed ceiling of silken sky, richly embroidered with stars. As they rained down, the threads that they trailed criss-crossed the sky with shimmering lines. When Tom finally tore his attention away from it and looked down again, he gasped out loud. For there was...

"The King," Pigsticker announced, simply, but in a voice charged with emotion. "Here he has stood, waiting unseen, for all the long times since last his Queen was among us, and who can count the years since then?"

Tom stared in awe at the mythical stone. The stone that his father had sought so determinedly, had longed for so desperately and had never been able to find; the stone that had made a learned man question his learning – and even his sanity. Dark grey and glistening in the moonlight, tall and jagged; as it stood it radiated an immense, untameable strength and a deep, heavy longing. Just being in its presence made Tom's breath catch in his throat.

The warrior chief called out to the ranks of his people. As one, they faced the stone, bowed their heads and touched their hands to their hearts. Then they moved to form a circle around it, moving with sure steps, holding their torches high. The Gypsies, too, moved quietly into the circle, guided by the old fiddler and his elderly lady companion, shushing the excited youngsters and calming their animals with gentle sounds. The wild creatures gathered where they would; the young tumbling together, the full-grown alert and wary. The tiny and the timid tucked themselves into the grass, until they were invisible but for the glint of moonlight on their dark, beady eyes.

"Time," said Pigsticker to Tom and Gilbert, and he motioned them inside the circle, ready to take their place in whatever was about to begin.

Geraldine watched the strange goings-on from the edge of the clearing, happy for once not to be the centre of attention. Finding the pain from her blisters distracting, she bent down and clumsily unfastened the buttons of her boots; a difficult, finger-aching job without a buttonhook. As her stockinged feet gingerly touched the woodland floor, she was all at once so shocked that she lost her balance and stumbled awkwardly to her knees on the ground.

Oh! The earth is moving! No, not moving, exactly... what's the word? Throbbing? Beating? How utterly strange!

It felt like a heart, like a drum, muffled but strong. And even more strangely, it began to feel good – soothing, somehow, pleasant and strong. Suddenly, Geraldine found that she wanted to lie down, right down there on the grass, with not even a blanket to keep her white dress from the dirt. Within moments, the squire's daughter would not have recognised herself, lolling on the bare earth, breathing the fresh night-time air and basking in a feeling of well-being she had never known before.

From the edges of the circle, many eyes watched as the ritual began. A single voice spoke out, high and clear and strong.

I say! It's that old fortune teller! But she looks different... younger, maybe... certainly better. I prefer that cloak to her horrible old shawl... maybe the magpie's gone now... I hope so...

Then Geraldine's thoughts were swept from her mind, as the Gypsy woman's call was answered by the whole crowd chanting as one. The rich, wild sound was something she had never heard before and it sent waves of shivers through her whole body. She noted that Tom and Gilbert stood motionless. Their friend the old man seemed to be talking to them at times, while the badger-hooded warrior chief stood between them and the stone, as if he would stop anyone who came too close.

This is like something from a book of myths and legends. Most peculiar, but... but...

Geraldine gave up trying to think and simply sighed with pleasure.

Inside the circle, Tom's impression of the proceedings was quite different. He felt tense, excited, edgy; as if he were balancing on a taut wire that hummed beneath his feet. When he heard the words that the young-old lady spoke, it was as if they flowed into his mind like a fast-running stream. But then, in contrast, the answering chanting broke over him like waves in the sea, leaving him shaking, breathless and strangely moved. For somewhere in that chorus came a sound he had not heard for many years; his mother's voice, soft and distant, and he struggled against the urge to cry out to her in return.

But then, like a rock or island providing a resting place in a turbulent sea, Pigsticker's warm, earthy tones would cut in with a word of comfort or a brief explanation, and Tom would breathe freely again, until the next time.

Finally, suddenly, the chanting halted; but long after the sound had ceased the air remained disturbed and unquiet, quivering with a silent echo. To Tom's surprise, the magpie Kapchak suddenly flew out of one of the tall trees and perched imperiously on the top of the standing stone – the only one, it seemed, permitted to touch it. He opened his black beak and Tom half expected him to speak in words. But all that came was his usual 'Kaark!' an odd sound, half-comical, half-ominous.

The vibration in the air promptly stopped, and stillness was restored. The magpie opened his wings and glided from his high perch onto the young-old lady's shoulder. She laughed and petted him, and the tension was broken. Relieved, Tom looked up at Pigsticker.

"What happens now?" he asked in a loud whisper.

"Watch," the old man replied.

What happened next was twofold. The younger members of the Gypsy clans gathered near the centre of the circle, led there by Willow with Rosebay and Darkus stepping proudly at her side. The old fiddler called several of his people around him and Tom saw that they carried their musical instruments. As the brightly dressed, excited youngsters took their places, Tom realised what was about to happen.

"Dancing!" he exclaimed.

The music began with the soft, gentle tones of a low whistle, playing a sad and beautiful tune, while the dancers simply swayed together, as graceful as young trees moving in a warm summer breeze. Then, one by one, the other instruments came in – a higher-pitched whistle, a fiddle and drum – and the music changed to a lively dance tune. The dancers began to skip and twirl, forming twos and fours and weaving in and out in time with the drum. Those watching began to clap and then to stamp, as the strong, wild rhythm took hold of them all.

Clapping and bobbing along with the music, Tom suddenly noticed that one part of the dance was often repeated – the dancers would form a ring, circle and turn, then break apart from each other, only to stand still for a fraction of a beat before spinning away to join up again. Every time, they formed a familiar jagged circle and tail. The pattern that had been marked on the earth and drawn across the sky was now brought to life by the energy and skill of the young Gypsy dancers.

Tom was breathless when the youngsters finally came to a halt. He felt as if he had danced every step himself. Gilbert, by contrast, hardly seemed to have noticed the spectacle, for he was still engrossed in his stone. Seeing this, Tom's smile left his face and he began to worry a little.

It must be time soon, time for him to give it up. Will he be able to do it? Will he be all right?

"Don't think on that, Master Thomas," advised Pigsticker, moving close to Tom as the dancers and crowd began to draw back together and grow quiet again. "Just look."

He gestured towards the edges of the circle, where the light from the torches gave way to the dark of the wood.

"They is coming," he said, "the Old Ones."

"What old ones?" Tom asked, but, as usual, Pigsticker said nothing, leaving him to work it out for himself.

Deep silence fell again within the cathedral of trees. Tom strained his eyes to see into the darkness, to try to make out who was approaching. Gooseflesh prickled on his arms as he spotted a glimmer among the flickering shadows. A dark eye, at about the height of his own head, glinted redly in a torch's light. Slowly, more dark eyes appeared among the trees, some low down, some high, but all large and luminous. A stag, bearing a magnificent spread of antlers, was stepping cautiously up to the edge of the ring of light. When he was sure it was safe, he let his does follow, accompanied by their delicate, dappled fawns. The small herd took its place, looking to the great stone at the centre of the circle. Tom was amazed.

"I didn't know there were deer in this wood!" Tom whispered to Pigsticker.

"There aren't," the old man replied, giving Tom an unreadable look from beneath his bent hat brim. And with that, he pointed to other parts of the circle, and Tom, in disbelief, made out the lean, shaggy, grey shapes of two adult wolves, and then, the rounder, fuzzier outlines of three cubs, who boldly edged to the front and stood staring out at the assembly of humans and animals before them.

Then, startled by a loud screeching grunt, Tom turned to a point further round the circle, just in time to see a huge, dark pig shape emerge from among the trees. Wild boar! Tall and black and fierce it stood, its back hunched, its tusks gleaming dangerously in the torchlight. A brood of noisy young came with him, jostling and butting each other in play. Their squeals were answered by a strange, rumbling yawn; when Tom saw that it came from the deep chest of a huge, brown bear, his mouth fell slowly open, and he had no words to say.

Gilbert, his hands firm upon the stone, turned to Tom and Pigsticker.

"It should be now," he stated.

His voice was unusually urgent and not completely steady. Pigsticker simply nodded, trusting Gilbert's judgement. The warrior chief stepped forward, raised his hands and addressed his people; at once they all dropped to one knee on the earth with their eyes turned towards the King. Then Pigsticker spoke to the Gypsies, and the old lady who had led the chanting came to stand beside him and the chief. These three joined hands and, together, they began to speak, or chant, or sing.

Tom could not have said what meaning was in those words, or whether they were hymn or spell, poem or prayer. But the sound of them took a powerful hold on his heart and mind. Before he knew what was happening, he, like all of those around him, was joining in with the words, as if he had known them since the day he was born.

Gilbert, meanwhile, stood silent until the chanting ceased, one small tear running down his cheek.

"Thomas," he said, in a choking whisper, "it is time for her to leave, and I cannot take her. The proper hands are here, she says, but I cannot tell whose. Will you choose for her, and for me? For I find I have no idea at all."

Tom nodded in response, feeling the force of his brother's sadness. He looked around the circle, at the faces there; some he knew, some he had never known, young and old and in between – and all at once he had the answer. One pair of round eyes was looking straight back at him, and the choice became no choice at all. Tom beckoned, Tinman nodded and let go of a small hand, and Cobby came running, his eyes alight with excitement.

"Is it me?" the little boy asked, a huge grin on his face.

"It is," Tom told him, smiling back, and Gilbert heard. "So be it," he said.

Four summers old, little Cobby stood, holding out his hands. As Gilbert laid the stone in them, the boy staggered under the weight, but he gathered all his strength to hold on. Gilbert flickered a faint, sad smile, then closed his eyes, twisting his hands tightly together. Uncertain what else to do, Tom put his hand on Cobby's shoulder and went with him as he walked, small and fearless, up to the warrior chief. All eyes watched him as he stood at the foot of the King Stone.

Close to, the surface of the King Stone was not as smooth as it looked from a distance. It looked aged and roughened, pitted and pocked with scratches and holes. Searching its surface, Tom spotted a niche high up on the rock – carved or natural, he could not tell, but in a most familiar shape.

"It goes in there, I think," he whispered to Cobby.

With an effort, Tom lifted the boy and the stone, hefting them almost onto his shoulder. Cobby reached upward with the stone in both hands, his little arms straining as he stretched as high as he could. Then, with a jolt, the stone seemed to shift by itself, to lock into the space that had waited for it, sinking in and settling as if pulled and held fast by a powerful magnet. Cobby let it go, and it stayed there, as if permanently joined, merged.

As this happened, Tom staggered backwards and he and Cobby fell to the ground in a tangle, for the King Stone seemed at once to burst into unexpected life. Its whole surface crackled and sparked, and the air around it started to buzz with warmth and life, glowing yellow as sunlight. With it came a ferocious, joyful energy which overtook all those near to the stone and then spread through the company in rippling, surging waves.

In the first burst of energy, pandemonium reigned. Touched by the stone's power, people and animals danced and ran; they jumped and pranced and rolled on the ground. Strangers hugged each other and raised their voices in wild cries, while above them the stars rained down ever harder and more brightly. The light from the glowing stone grew stronger by the moment. When it reached the level of daylight, birdsong rang out all around and bees and butterflies flew in clouds around the revellers' heads. Kapchak, his feathers shining and whole, flew wild aerial acrobatics overhead, adding his raucous calls to the chorus.

Kapchak was not the only one who appeared miraculously younger – as Tom moved in a daze through the crowd, he could have sworn that he saw Tinman and Willow dancing, somehow a young lad and a blushing, giggling girl. Magister, a horse well on in years, frolicked like any excitable yearling. But when Tom came face to face with Rosebay and Darkus, and they swung him around as they had so often in the dance, their eyes were older – shaded by the wisdom that long life brings.

It was as if past and present and future had merged and flowed together, like the metal and stone and starlight which had become one in the Joining of the King Stone and its Queen.

Then, after a time, calm gradually descended, and all those present began to realise that the miraculous time was drawing to its close. The wild animals, last to arrive, had already crept away out of sight. There were many embraces exchanged in those minutes, between those who would see each other again and those who never would, new friends and old, comrades and strangers. Many small gifts and tokens were given and received. Tom found himself clutching a corn dolly made by Willow's clever fingers, and felt her wise, motherly eyes look into his very soul. He could make no reply, but Willow understood.

Then, swiftly, urgently, Tom ran to look for his friend the young rider. When he found him, the two exchanged hearty shoulder slaps one last time. The warrior lad drew a leather thong from round his neck, rolled it up and placed it in Tom's hand, clasping his own hand over them in a gesture both of friendship and farewell. Tom, searching for a gift to give in return, dug in his pockets and pulled out the string of sugar beads that he had won from the vicar's bran tub. His friend was at first mystified, then highly appreciative; then he turned and headed away, walking with his pony and the older lady warrior, and he did not once look back.

As the festivities drew to their close, four old friends

found each other and stood close, sharing the final moments of the shining hour.

"So, my friends," said Pigsticker, "we has done what we must, and done what we may. The King and his Queen are one again and the land is strengthened for what is to come. Though dark times shall break upon us, this land shall not be overrun."

"We must be thankful, then," said Tinman, with relief in his voice. Willow took his hand.

"We must," she said, "and for a time we may be glad. But we have not turned the tide; we cannot, and still it rushes in. A tide of fear and death it is, and many of our sons shall be lost to it, and our daughters left to wither alone."

She stared across the clearing at Cobby, tired now from importance and dancing, leaning sleepily against the faithful Senso. She sought out Rosebay and Darkus, who were arguing about who would lead Magister home. She watched Tom reach out to his brother and saw Gilbert's face lit by a rare and luminous smile. Her eyes filled with tears.

Curse the Knowing! For what use is it, if it tells only of sorrow?

Tinman held tightly to Willow's hand, for her words had filled him with fear.

After a long pause, Mother Bessamy spoke.

"True are your words, as ever, Willow," she said, "and rightly you warn that many hard days are to come. But we have done all that is asked of us. We have summoned what spirit we may from elder days in defence of this land, and we have set the foot upon the path. It is for others, now, to do their part. One from this night shall go onward, taking with him all our hopes, and it is for the black-hoods to find him and do what is needful. We can do no more."

So saying, Mother Bessamy drew on her clay pipe, and the soft smoke drifted into the air, leaving its bittersweet scent behind.

Black-hoods! Why them? Why must we trust to those meddling fools? It would be better if they had never come to this land.

Willow read her man's thoughts from his face.

"We must because we must," she said softly, looking deeply into his eyes, "for it is the Way. The older Laws give way to the Bell and the Book. So it has been, so it shall be. We cannot change the Pattern, my love."

Tinman slumped slightly, knowing that it would be useless to argue.

And so the four stood together, their world secure around them, for a while.

Moments later, the very last of the light faded away. The final sight which Tom saw before complete darkness fell was Geraldine, standing in her stockings at the edge of the circle, her camera dangling from her hand and a ridiculous smile on her face.

CHAPTER 18

Tom felt a hard lump dig painfully into his back. He groaned and his eyes flickered open, then closed again as they met cool, grey light. He reached down for his blanket, but his groping hand found nothing to hold. Groaning again, he rubbed one arm across his face, trying to clear away the fog of sleep.

Ow... my back... this bed is... oh!

With a start, he realised that there was no bed. His eyes opened wide, and he saw green branches above his head, the canvas of his tent nowhere to be seen.

Fully awake now, Tom sat up sharply and stared around, feeling most peculiar. He was in the wood, uncomfortably couched among the roots of a tree. A few feet away, Gilbert lay snoring, flat on his back with his head on a mound of moss. Even stranger, Geraldine Montfalcon was lying under the tree next to Tom's, curled in a tight ball, clutching her footwear like a favourite doll. Tom's brain reeled and he rubbed his head hard, leaving his hair sticking up in messy tufts.

What is going on here?

Tom hauled himself to his feet, grimacing at the chilliness of his dew-damp clothes. He went and knelt beside Gilbert, saying his name softly, over and over again. This was the only way to wake him without sending him into a panic, but it took time. Slowly, memories of the night's drama came back to Tom's mind, bringing with them both a sense of wonder and a gnawing disquiet. It was morning, albeit very early, and his father would know that he and Gilbert had not returned to the camp.

Oh no… Geraldine didn't get home either… we could be in serious trouble for that… and… oh, oh no… did I really break into her house? What if… ?

Eventually, Gilbert opened his eyes, interrupting Tom's panicky thoughts. He frowned as he looked at his brother, on his knees in the grass, and made as if to speak.

"Oh," he said, "I find that I do not know the date."

"Never mind the date," Tom said, "Gil, we have a serious problem. We're stuck out in the wood somewhere and we have to get back – and we've got to get Geraldine home as well, or her father might think she's been stolen away, or something, and we'll get the blame."

Gilbert sat up, blinking.

"Yes, indeed, quite possibly," he commented after a moment's thought, looking over at the girl's still-sleeping form. "I suggest that you wake her," he said, in his usual serious tone. Then he added, slyly, "and tell her to put her boots on when she goes dreaming."

As he spoke, Tom saw his mouth twitch into a brief smile. Amazed to see his brother finding humour in their situation, he found that he, too, suddenly saw it as hilarious, and burst into laughter. The sound woke Geraldine, and, though confused and rather embarrassed, she came straight to the point.

"You two have clearly gone mad, once and for all," she stated. "I, for one, do not make a habit of this kind of nonsense, so I must look to you… experts, for guidance. Where are we, and why, and how do we get home?"

Neither Tom nor Gilbert had an answer to offer, and they looked around helplessly. The regal avenue of trees and the King Stone were nowhere to be seen. All around, the early morning light revealed ordinary oaks, beeches and birches and humbler bushes, standing as they always had. Among the branches, a few birds piped the last notes of the dawn chorus. No path was visible and no familiar landmark presented itself. They were truly lost.

Geraldine stood up, frowning at the pink stains on her crumpled skirt, now overlaid with smears of green from the grass.

"We require a guide," she observed.

Immediately, as if in reply, there was a rustle in the branches of one of the nearby hazels. A black-and-white bundle fluttered clumsily down out of it to land in an untidy, tailless heap between the feet of Tom and Gilbert.

"Kapchak!" exclaimed Tom, delighted.

Was it just part of last night's lingering strangeness, or did the magpie give him a meaningful look? A suggestion of an idea flitted into his mind and he decided to give it a try.

"Kapchak," he began, politely, "we are rather lost. Would you be so kind as to show us the way home?"

"For heaven's sake, Tommy!" Geraldine moaned. "You're talking to a bird now. *A bird.*"

But then, unexpectedly, she gave a short laugh and pulled on her boots, though she quickly gave up on trying to fasten them properly and just left them open. As the magpie hopped and flapped away, she rolled her eyes, but followed him anyway. After a surprisingly short time, Tom realised that he was on a familiar path, and knew he could find his way back. Kapchak fluttered off in the opposite direction and Tom called out thanks to him as he went. Then, as they approached the edge of the camp, all the three youngsters paused to peer at the sight before them, crouching in the bushes so as not to be seen.

Oh. Father is asleep in his chair. Father is asleep and the Reverend Pilcher is also sleeping, on the chair next to him. Father's hat is over his eyes and Reverend Pilcher's spectacles are on, but have slipped. I do not believe that they meant to sleep outdoors. The other man is Mr Montfalcon, who is snoring quite loudly. I do not believe that he makes a habit of sleeping outdoors either. I suspect that he came here to search for Geraldine. She is here. Will he be happy or angry or confused – or something else?

Tom's voice, whispering faintly, interrupted Gilbert's thoughts.

"What do you think we should do?" he asked.

Geraldine opened her mouth to reply. But then she stopped, frozen, and simply pointed instead. A pair of eyes had opened and was peering blearily in their direction. The owner of the eyes was rising, with an effort, from one of the chairs. They heard a sharp crack as stiff knees straightened, then watched helplessly as slow steps brought the figure closer and closer to their hiding place.

There was to be no escape, and, knowing it, all three slowly stood up. Tom stared at the ground, mortified. When he finally dared to peek upwards, the eyes that had spied them were staring back down at him, spectacles now pushed firmly back into place.

"Praise be to God," whispered Reverend Pilcher, closing his eyes and smiling broadly with relief. "The prodigals are returned, safe and sound. God be thanked."

Then he held a finger to his lips, cutting off any reply.

"Let us wake your fathers," he said softly, "and may I suggest an old adage? *Least said, soonest mended.*"

And so, with the vicar smoothing the ruffled feathers of the Professor and the squire, the return to camp was managed with a minimum of fuss. Professor Warrington barked a little, but then came forward and, for the first time in Tom's memory, gathered his sons into an ungainly embrace. Then, fearing he might have offended Gilbert, he let go suddenly and stepped back with a gruff apology, only to stumble and fall backwards into his chair. Oddly, rather than being angry, he laughed. Tom joined in, Reverend Pilcher began to giggle, and a brighter mood took hold. Even Gilbert smiled slightly as he straightened his waistcoat and said a polite good morning to his father.

Mr Montfalcon, meanwhile, was clutching Geraldine tightly to himself as she told a carefully garbled version of being lost in the woods and found and brought back by Tom and Gilbert. Tom noted how skilfully she stopped his questions with a few well-placed tears. Then, Mr Montfalcon shook hands with both the brothers and thanked them over and over again.

"My wife would never have forgiven me," he admitted quietly to Reverend Pilcher, "if anything had happened to Baby."

At this moment, the party was joined by Arthur, Cedric, Wilfred and John, who had been searching the woods all night. Seeing that the boys were back, John let out a whoop and ran across the camp, where he rugby-tackled Tom.

"Where have you been, you rascal?" he shouted, then stood up hurriedly, saying, "Sorry, sir," to the Professor, as if he were at school.

This sent his fellow workers, and Tom, into further rounds of laughter. All four started to talk at once about the night's events.

It transpired that they had met with the Professor and a panicked Mr Montfalcon and heard that that the boys and Geraldine were missing. They had immediately formed a search party and looked everywhere they could think of around the village and the camp, then gone into the wood to search further. They had walked and walked and looked and called and become more and more confused.

"I would swear," announced Arthur, "that that wood was ten times the size I thought it was…"

"But we just seemed to go round in circles," Cedric cut in, "as if we were on a track and couldn't get off it…"

Then John snorted with laughter once more.

"Cedric reckons he saw a bear!" he chortled, pointing at him and giggling helplessly.

"I did!" protested Cedric, but Arthur was having none of it.

"You saw the bottom of too many cider flagons, I reckon," he declared.

Mention of drink brought on thoughts of food. Gilbert, who had been rather quiet, suddenly remembered something.

"My cake!" he exclaimed. "What happened to my cake?"

"I brought it back for you," said Reverend Pilcher, and he disappeared into the Professor's tent, to return carrying the cake in its box.

"We should eat it now," Gilbert suggested.

Once Tom had started up the reluctant stove and got the old blackened kettle on the boil, there was soon strong tea to go with the cake. Reverend Pilcher kept the conversation flowing as they sat around eating, and competently steered it away from the subject of what had actually happened during the night, for which Tom was extremely grateful.

Then, suddenly, the Professor pointed at Tom.

"Thomas!" he exclaimed. "Where did you get that?'

Tom's hand went to his throat, where, to his surprise, he felt a leather thong with a small piece of metal attached.

"Oh, I, er… found it in the wood," he improvised, trying to remember when he had tied his friend's gift around his neck.

"Show it to me," commanded the Professor.

When Tom took off the charm on its leather thong and handed it over, his father's eyes began to glow with a kind of excitement which Tom had seen many times before.

"I do believe…" he began, "… if this is what I think it is… then we may be on the cusp of a truly major discovery! Well spotted, young Thomas! You must show me exactly where you found this, and Pilcher, old friend, we must think again about this site's date, and its purpose, come to that!"

"And I will leave you to it," said Mr Montfalcon, hastily, beginning to heave his bulk up from the low camp chair, "for I must take my daughter home and make sure that she is duly cared for."

And so, after a further round of handshakes and thanks, Geraldine and her father started walking slowly towards the road, where the car and its faithful driver would be waiting for them. As Geraldine limped away, she looked back at Tom. If he had not known her better, he would have sworn that she gave him a conspirator's wink. He added it to the many mysteries lying unsolved in his mind, all of which, he suddenly found, he was far too tired to think about.

EPILOGUE

It was a parting of rather unlikely friends. Tom sat with Geraldine on the same fallen tree where he had talked with Pigsticker several weeks before. Since the night of the pageant they had struck up a wary companionship, nobody else being able or willing to discuss it and to try to work out what it all could have meant.

Gilbert had returned doggedly to his work, saying little. Tom had recognised this as his brother's way of steadying his mind and heart after all the upheavals of his time as Finder. There was a change in him, though. Although he was still mostly his serious self, he had begun to laugh a little more often, particularly at Geraldine's questions about the archaeological site. She seemed to have gained a genuine interest in the dig, but then, as the Professor had remarked, gold had a way of doing that to a person.

For, certainly, gold had been among the finds which the ground had finally begun to give up. The Professor had asked Tom to point out where he had found the charm which he wore round his neck and, although Tom had chosen the spot completely at random, it had proved to be very rich indeed. The best of the finds were a gold hare the size of a matchbox and a brooch of silver wire, Welsh work, which the Professor reckoned had been abandoned after a skirmish with the Saxons, sometime around the 7th Century.

The Professor was delighted with the finds, even though they threw no particular light on the nature of the stone circle, which seemed determined to remain as mysterious as ever. But at least when he took the objects to the University, his colleagues and rivals had not hidden their envy. He had been in a much better temper ever since.

Tom often toyed with the small talisman which the young grey-hooded warrior had given to him. It was a curved shape, rather suggestive of a windswept, racing horse, made from hammered and smoothed metal. The feeling of it had become so familiar under his fingers that Tom felt that he had owned it all his life. Perhaps the Professor had noticed that it had meaning for him, for he had not taken it to be boxed up, labelled and added to the growing hoard of finds. Instead, he left it in his son's keeping and mentioned it no more.

Geraldine had visited the site daily since the night of the Pageant and the ritual and, between Tom's errands, the two had gone over and over the events they had witnessed. Their countless questions and suggestions had brought them no closer to understanding the meaning of all that had happened. How had the King Stone appeared and disappeared overnight? Where had the warriors come from and where were they now? How had Pigsticker and the fortune teller known so much about a ritual that, if the old story was to be believed, only went on once in a hundred years or more?

The animals – the 'old ones' as Pigsticker had called them – remained a tantalising mystery to Tom. Several times he had walked in the woods, on increasingly quiet feet, hoping to catch a glimpse of the shy deer. They had remained elusive, but he could sometimes almost feel their silent presence somewhere nearby. Standing quiet and dreamy in the woods, he would listen to the gentle sound of bees and conjure tall, graceful figures from the dappled sun falling on the leaves.

I wish I could see them one more time...

Now, sitting on the tree trunk, Tom belatedly realised that Geraldine was speaking.

"So," she continued, as Tom made sure that his face showed polite interest, "I realised that he is petrified of what I might tell Mama when I arrive in Paris on Thursday... She would not enjoy hearing that I was left alone among all the unwashed loons and ruffians at the Pageant and then enticed into the wood, lost and alone, wandering unguarded, at the mercy of Gypsies, wolves, madmen and bears for a whole, long night..."

"Steady on," said Tom, giving her a sidelong look, "that's a tall story. This is just a normal English wood. There's nothing to be afraid of here, so long as you stay away from the nettles, brambles – and warriors from another age who want to roast you on a spit. And, don't forget, it was one of those Gypsies who led us to you. If it hadn't been for him, things would have been a lot worse..."

Geraldine was trying not to smile, for she loved to bait Tom with remarks about the Gypsies. In reality, she had begun to gain a little respect for them, though she was certainly not going to show it.

"Tommy," Miss Montfalcon continued, rolling her eyes, "if you will let me continue, I am about to tell you something which you may like to hear. Though if you would prefer to argue, please do so..."

"No, no, do go on," Tom urged her, airily, putting up his hands in mock surrender and refusing to be drawn.

"I was about to tell you," she went on, in her schoolmistress tone, "that Papa and I have made a pact. I will not tell Mama about his terrible neglect of my welfare, and I can have anything which I choose in return."

She preened slightly and Tom offered a tight-lipped smile in reply.

"Lucky you," he replied, "what will you choose? A diamond tiara? A castle? The hand of a prince in marriage?"

"Actually," she interrupted, "I have already chosen. I have made him swear on his life that he will never cut down this wood, and that if he must build a road, he will keep it far away from the trees and the stone circle. Yes…" she trailed off with sigh, "… my first ever noble gesture. And probably my last, if the truth be told."

Did I hear that properly? Did she just say…

Geraldine smiled wryly, relishing the thunderstruck look on Tom's face.

"Tell Gilbert and your father for me, will you?" she asked. "I have to go now. I must make sure that my packing is being done properly, to be certain that I will look my best for Mama."

She jumped down off the log and walked off, leaving Tom standing, amazed.

When he recovered his wits, Tom scrambled after the red-haired girl, now making her way towards the road. As he drew level with her, she held out her bag for him to carry, treating him as a servant. For once, Tom made no protest.

"Are you looking forward to seeing your mother,

then?" he asked, as they walked through the field, down the slope to the road.

"Oh yes," Geraldine replied, "I suppose I do miss her while she's away. Though, I have to say, Papa is rather easier to fool..."

"It's odd, you know," said Tom, thoughtfully, "my father never used to speak about our mother at all. I hardly knew her, because I was only little when she died. But since that night, he's started talking about her, telling us stories about her. It turns out she was really funny and liked pranks and things. She used to teach Reverend Pilcher to say words in Welsh, only they were actually rude things that would get him into trouble, and he didn't know. I can't imagine Father being with somebody like that, but he was mad about her, so the Pilchard says."

Geraldine nodded approvingly.

"I love visiting Aunt Miranda, that's Mama's sister, in Paris," she said. "Mother goes there every summer, and I always join them for a while before returning to school. We go to the shops and we promenade, and there are shows and *soirées* and it's never, ever boring. But..." she added, "the best of it is, Mama and Aunt have something dreadful to say about absolutely everybody. The girls at school love it, when I tell them all about it."

"School," repeated Tom, hearing the word as the death knell of summer. Then he brightened. "Perhaps Father will forget to send me back again this year," he said.

This had happened only once, when the Professor had become completely carried away on a dig in Greece, but Tom lived in constant hope of the error being repeated.

"I'll see that he's reminded," said Geraldine.

When they reached the road, the car was ready and waiting. The driver, Wilson, greeted Tom kindly. Twice, now, the squire had taken the boys for rides in the car, and Wilson had enjoyed their sensible questions and their obvious enjoyment of the marvellous machine. But today it was only Geraldine who climbed into the leather seats and settled herself in. Then she remembered something, and opened up her bag.

"Here," she said, handing a small packet to Tom, "I thought you might like these. Photographs of the dig. Sadly," she added, "the ones from *you know when* didn't work out at all, just came out black, even though it was quite light at one point, as you will recall. One of the other pictures has a strange white smear on it, but the rest are fine, in fact, rather good, if I do say so myself."

Tom thanked her as she signalled to the driver to set off home. She looked down at Tom, and a cat's smile flickered on her face.

"Goodbye, Tommy," she said, "or should I say, *au revoir.*"

The car rumbled into life and pulled away. As Geraldine turned to wave, Tom had just enough wit to call, "Goodbye, Baby!" and to enjoy her outraged look, for she had made it very clear that this name was utterly forbidden.

Tom waved until the car was out of sight and then turned to trudge back up the slope towards the common and the archaeological site, for the team was busy and he was needed. The air was cooler now, the sky littered with scraps of cloud that scudded along on the breeze. The weather had broken with storms almost immediately after the night of the ritual, and now, when Tom picked a stalk of grass to chew on, it was fresh and green with a good, wild taste.

When he reached the stile, Tom couldn't resist pausing to open Geraldine's packet of photographs and take a first look through them. He smiled at the one of John's startled face when he dropped the bag of soil in the pit, and grudgingly admired the quite artistic nature of some of the prints. There was a particularly fine one of the Professor, looking fierce and oddly heroic, holding a yardstick just as if it were a sword. But when he came to the print that was marred by the white blur, it caught his interest immediately, and he stopped to stare at it.

What is that? It can't be…

On the surface, it was an ordinary enough picture. Two of the stones, the edge of the deep pit and Tom himself, looking at something which he was holding in his hands. Beyond that, the edge of the wood, with leaves in sun and shadow, making dappled shades of grey. There, in amongst the bushes and leaves, were the odd marks that had dismayed the photographer. They looked like scratches on the print, white scrapes forming a loose 'v', with darker blurs between them. In themselves, they didn't look like anything, but what caught Tom's eye was a shape in the shadows below the marks.

Tom looked hard at the picture and held it at arm's length, trying to make out what, if anything, he could see. Yes, there was definitely something. By squinting, he found that he could just pick out a figure, blending into the leaves, hard to spot but unmistakable once seen.

They're not faults in the photograph at all! Could it be... no, surely not... is it?.

There it was. A headdress of badger-skin, exactly like that worn by the chief of the King's warriors. But this figure was not he. It was not so tall, and stood quite differently, not like a warrior, but rather, a watcher.

It is!

"Pigsticker!" exclaimed Tom aloud.

"At your service."

Tom whirled around. There was the old man, standing behind him, unobtrusive as ever in his earth-coloured clothes and his shapeless felt hat. He peered at the photographs held in Tom's hands.

"Pictures, hmm," he remarked, "they can tell you so much, I suppose, but me, I prefers a good story. What do you say, Master Thomas?"

"I don't know what to say," Tom admitted, with a lopsided smile. "With everything that's gone on, my head's still spinning. How did it all happen? What did it mean? Was it real? That stone – how did it... you know... and where is it now? Where did the warriors come from, and where did they go? And the animals, too? Why do things feel so different now? And how did you get into this picture?"

He ran out of breath, and Pigsticker stood silently, his eyes twinkling under the brim of his hat.

"Questions," he began thoughtfully, "is best dealt with one at a time. Close your eyes, Master Thomas, and clear your head, and choose the one you most wants an answer to, for that's the way to start, to my way of thinking."

Tom was delighted that, at last, it looked as though

Pigsticker might throw light on some of the mysteries of the past few weeks. Smiling, he followed the old Gypsy's advice.

What shall I ask… ?

As he closed his eyes, a rush of images flashed through his mind – like a series of photographs, only coloured, vivid, real. The King Stone and the cathedral of trees in the forest; the grinning young warrior and his excitable horse; the glow in the air when the stone sprang into life; the wild eyes of the wolf and the boar; Gilbert's face, lit by joy, with the stars raining down from above. He took a deep breath, then another, as he lost himself in reliving many, many moments – of fear and delight, of excitement and panic and exhilaration and awe. Amidst it all, he waited and waited for one clear question to arise in his mind. Finally, it came.

Yes! That's it! I've got it!

But when he opened his eyes and blinked in the light, he saw that the old man was gone. He put a hand to his brow and scanned all around, searching for any sign of him, finding none.

"Pigsticker!" shouted Tom, into the empty air. "*Who are you?*"

But no answer came, only the flick of a badger's tail away in the distance, as it slipped into the bushes and disappeared.

ACKNOWLEDGEMENTS

My appreciation, first and foremost, to Nick for the inspiration, guidance and encouragement that made this book possible.

Thanks to Ajay Kumar for initial cover designs.

The following also gave invaluable support: Bev Mason, Wendy Furgusson, Leonie Stokes, John Edwards and, of course, my wonderful Mum. I am most grateful to you all.